FOREVER AND

Riverbend, Texas Heat 4

Marla Monroe

MENAGE EVERLASTING

Siren Publishing, Inc.
www.SirenPublishing.com

A SIREN PUBLISHING BOOK
IMPRINT: Ménage Everlasting

FOREVER AND ALWAYS
Copyright © 2012 by Marla Monroe

ISBN: 978-1-62242-242-5

First Printing: December 2012

Cover design by Les Byerley
All art and logo copyright © 2012 by Siren Publishing, Inc.

PUBLISHER
Siren Publishing, Inc.
www.SirenPublishing.com

FOREVER AND ALWAYS

Riverbend, Texas Heat 4

MARLA MONROE
Copyright © 2012

Chapter One

Lana Peters rested her pounding head against the steering wheel once she had parked the car in the parking lot. She was hot, tired, and ready to go home. She didn't want to spend the next five hours on her feet dishing burgers to flighty teenagers and grouchy parents with screaming kids. She opened her eyes and sighed. As much as she hated this job, it helped pay her bills. She still had another four months of payments before she was free and clear of her school loans. Then she could start to back off of the second job.

Despite having a decent job as an administrative assistant at the local high school, Lana had to work the part-time gig at the local fast-food joint to help pay off her student loans. Even though she kept telling herself that once she had the loan paid off she would quit her second job, the reality was that she needed a newer car, one she would be able to depend on during the upcoming winter months. The only way she would be able to afford that would be to continue working at the fast-food job.

"You coming in or sitting out in the car all night?"

Lana jumped then grinned. Leave it to Joseph to startle her.

"I'm coming. What are you doing out here? Taking a break?"

"Picking up trash. Not much going on right now. Better hurry in before you're late."

She nodded and locked up the car before heading toward the entrance in the back. With Joseph outside, the door would be propped open. She slipped in the back way and punched in before Rick caught her. He didn't like for them to come in that way. He wanted to know when they showed up. She adjusted her name badge as she stepped up front to locate her duty schedule for the night.

"Hey, Lana. You're drive-thru tonight. Dee is sick." Rick tossed her the drive-thru keys and headset.

She grimaced. She hated working drive-thru. That meant she would close the window and not get home much before 1:00 a.m. *Remember, more money to pay bills.* Reminding herself didn't do a lot of good when her head already hurt and her feet ached.

She got to work, and by the time midnight hit and she could lock up the window for good, Lana was near tears. Her headache had morphed into a full-blown neck and shoulder ache as well. Her back and legs were useless noodles that threatened to fold on her at any given minute. She quickly cleaned up the area and counted down her drawer. For once she was right on the money and wouldn't be filling out any extra paperwork.

"You ready to walk out?" Joseph asked when she emerged from the bathroom a few minutes later.

"Yeah. I've already clocked out. Let's go."

She followed Joseph to her car and waved him off when she was safely locked inside. She jabbed the key into the ignition and turned, expecting it to crank right up. Instead, she got nothing. It didn't even make a clicking sound.

"God, not tonight. Please!" She tried again with the same result.

By that time, the parking lot was empty except for Rick's pickup truck parked by the back door. She really didn't want to have to walk across the empty parking lot to bang on the back door and ask for his help. He would take it the wrong way. He had been trying to get her to go out with him for months. She'd thought she had managed to convince him that she wasn't interested, but that might all change if she ended up asking him for help.

She looked up and down the street in front of her. It was essentially empty. Her apartment was only a little over a mile away. She could walk that in only few minutes, right? Nothing ever happened around Riverbend, Texas. She would be fine. Glancing one last time at Rick's pickup, Lana made up her mind and climbed out of the car. She grabbed her backpack purse and locked up the car. It wasn't as if there was anything worth stealing in it. Just habit, she guessed.

The first few minutes of walking proved to be the worst. She jerked at every sound in the night air. Her legs and feet seemed made of lead, taking a monumental effort to get them to move. Eventually, she calmed down enough that by the time she was halfway home, she wondered why she hadn't saved gas and walked to and from work before.

A dark-colored car pulled up beside her and the window rolled down.

"Need a ride?"

Lana didn't recognize the voice, so she didn't turn to look into the car. "No, thanks. I'm almost home now." She walked a little closer to the buildings on her right.

"Nonsense. You're still a long ways from home. Let me give you a ride."

She shook her head and realized she was beginning to shake all over now. She didn't know whoever this was, but they acted as if they knew her. The car pulled a little ahead of her and stopped in her path. She panicked, unable to move to save her life. Just as the driver's side door opened on the car, a truck pulled up behind her.

"Lana, come on. You should have waited when your car wouldn't start."

She recognized the voice but couldn't remember the man's name. He and his brother had stopped by that night for burgers in the drive-thru. She saw them several times a week picking up something to eat. Did she trust him or the man she didn't recognize at all?

Lana didn't hesitate. She turned and walked back toward the truck where someone stepped out of the passenger side and held the door open for her. She let him help her into the front seat. Then she was forced to slide toward the middle when the man slipped in next to her.

"Easy, Lana. No one's going to hurt you. Just relax. We'll get you home." The driver smiled down at her.

All she could do was nod as she gazed into his amazing hazel eyes. Then the other man spoke next to her, jerking her head around.

"I'm Justin, and this is my brother Paul. Are you okay?"

"Y–Yes. Thanks for stopping. I don't know what I would have done."

"You shouldn't have walked, Lana. Why didn't you ask Rick for help?" Paul's voice was pitched much lower than Justin's.

"I didn't want Rick to read anything into it. He's been asking me out a lot."

"That boy knows better than to push someone."

"Paul, do you blame him?" Justin's quick grin wasn't lost on her.

"Um, I live over in the Ivy, building three."

"We know where you live, Lana. You shouldn't be working so late at night living where you do. It's not safe at night to come and go." It was obvious that Paul didn't approve of where she lived. Why that mattered to her, she didn't know. She barely knew the two men.

"This is the first time I've had any trouble. I plan to get a new car, so it won't happen again."

"Good. I hate to think of you out here without someone to watch out for you. Like Paul said, it's dangerous." Justin's arm was stretched out behind her on the back of the seat.

She was relieved when they pulled into her apartment complex that he hadn't let it drape across her shoulders. She just didn't feel comfortable around them. It wasn't a scared kind of uncomfortable. It was more of an awareness that caught her off guard. Paul pulled up in her parking place as if he knew exactly where it was. Then he turned and watched as Justin pulled back and opened the door to let her out of the truck.

"I'll walk her up to her apartment. Be right back."

"Oh, you don't have to do that." Lana finally got her wits back about her and started to ease out of the truck. She was surprised when Justin lifted her from the seat at her waist and gently set her on the ground.

"I know, but I don't want to leave without knowing you're safely locked up in your apartment."

She shrugged and led the way upstairs to her third-story home, unlocking the door and stepping inside before he could stop her.

"Thanks for giving me the ride. Tell Paul I said thanks, too."

"I'll do that. Now close the door and lock it for me. I want to hear the locks click."

Lana frowned, but stepped back into the gloom of the room and closed the door, making sure to click each lock in place. Then she stood there waiting for some sign that Justin was still on the other side of the door. When she heard a truck pull out of the parking lot below, she knew he was indeed gone. Oddly enough, her headache was gone, all but a memory, and she no longer felt totally alone and frightened. It was as if some part of Paul and Justin was still residing inside her, keeping her company.

Paul's gorgeous hazel eyes and shaggy, rich brown hair complemented a masculine face with a square jaw and full, sensuous lips. There were lines at the corners of his eyes that probably came from squinting into the sun since he didn't have laugh lines at his mouth. He appeared to be the more serious of the two brothers. He struck her as trustworthy and solid, a good friend to have at your back during trouble.

She hadn't missed his rocking body, either. Broad shoulders and an equally wide chest tapered down to a narrow waist. She couldn't see him very well in the dimness of the truck's interior, but she had the impression he was muscular all over.

Justin's eyes twinkled when he smiled, and there were fine lines at the corners of both his mouth and his eyes as if he spent a lot of time smiling and laughing. He was lighter and less intimidating than his brother. His handsome body sported muscles that spoke of hard work, not gym time. He had chocolate-brown eyes with long, dark lashes and an amazing smile. His rich brown hair was pulled back and tied at the nape of his neck. At close to six feet two inches, he and his brother would probably be the same height. Next to her mere five foot three inches, Lana felt petite despite her well-rounded body.

She had no illusions about her size or appearance. She wasn't one to worry or angst over it. She had long since come to accept her body and didn't try to apologize for it. Despite the men's kindness at giving her a ride and seeing her home safely, she knew it had been just that—a kindness. There was no way either one of them would be interested in someone like her. They were much too handsome and obviously financially secure by the looks of their new-looking Ford King Ranch truck.

At twenty-five, Lana had had her share of boyfriends, but there had been no one in the last two years. She was concentrating on getting herself out of debt from her college loans. Though she had a business degree with a double major in management and marketing, she had taken the job as an administrative assistant at the local high school to be near her mother as she fought pancreatic cancer.

It had been nearly six months since her mom's death, and she still missed her. Her father wasn't in the picture, having left when she was only four years old. Her mom had raised her on her own, and Lana felt she'd done a wonderful job. They hadn't had much, but she knew she was loved.

As much as Lana wanted a nice relaxing bath, she needed to shower off and get to bed instead. Tomorrow was Saturday and she worked closing again. She needed all the rest she could get because she still had her rebellious car to tend to as well as her Saturday chores.

Stepping into the hot, stinging spray, she moaned at the wonderful sensations pelting her tired muscles. Lana made short work of cleaning up and then just stood in the deluge of hot water until it began to cool. She grabbed a towel as she stepped out of the shower and quickly dried off before blow-drying her hair.

When she climbed into bed, she thought again about the two handsome men and wondered how they knew her so well. She didn't remember ever really talking to them that much. Sure, she had a name tag on her uniform that said *Lana*, but it was almost as if they already knew everything about her.

Despite that seeming odd when the stranger that had been in the car had known her name as well, Lana felt like she could trust Paul and Justin for some reason. The fact that they had seen her to her door without trying to take advantage of her spoke volumes, in her book. Too many times men tended to think they had an obligation to at least steal a kiss when around her. It was one of the reasons she hadn't dated in a while. The whole dating scene had become disillusioning to say the least. Besides, once her mom's cancer had gotten in the last stages, she hadn't had much time to devote to anyone other than her mom and, of course, her job.

Relaxing under the thin sheet in an effort to remain cool in the warm apartment, Lana wished her bills were all paid now so she could branch out some and enjoy herself for a change. Right now she was too exhausted to maintain a steady relationship, and she wasn't a one-night-stand sort of gal. *Maybe in a few more months.* She smiled at that thought and drifted off into sleep.

Chapter Two

"Any idea who the asshole was that was trying to get her in the car with them?" Paul asked as they pulled back out onto the street.

"Not a clue. I don't think I've ever seen that car around here before either, and there wasn't a license plate."

"We should probably tell Sheriff Tidwell about it tomorrow."

"Do you want to swing back by and see if we can tell what's wrong with her car?" Justin asked.

"Naw, we'll check it out tomorrow. As late as it is, she probably won't be up much before noon anyway. We can swing through on the way out to work and look at it."

Paul and his brother, Justin, owned a landscape business. They were working out on the Billups' ranch. The Burger Hop would be on the way to their house in the morning. They would stop and have a look at Lana's car on the way out there. He didn't like the suspicion that it had been tampered with creeping around in his head.

He looked over at his younger brother by barely a year. Justin was the more outgoing and loved women. The fact that once he'd seen Lana several months back he hadn't wanted to date anyone wasn't lost on him. Hell, he pretty much felt the same way. She called to him on a level that no one else ever had before. It both thrilled and terrified him. That someone could have that much power over him stole his breath.

"I sure don't like that she lives in that roach-infested place. The place is a death trap."

Paul winced. He agreed with Justin, but they couldn't do anything about it yet. First they had to win her trust, and then they would talk her into moving in with them. Everything took time and planning. Unfortunately, he felt like they didn't have a lot of time to spare.

"We'll get her out of it soon."

"She shouldn't have to work two jobs, either. She deserves to be coddled and pampered."

Paul couldn't help the half smile that statement brought out. He happened to agree with him wholeheartedly. Still, it would take time to convince Lana to give it up and let them take care of her. She was a proud little thing.

From the top of her glorious mane of rich auburn hair that she kept pulled back in a ponytail to the tips of her painted toenails, Lana demanded respect. Her curvy body kept his cock hard and at attention anytime she was around. More and more, just the thought of her pale porcelain skin with its dusting of freckles was enough to elicit a full-fledged hard-on.

Deep blue eyes in a heart-shaped face missed nothing. He longed to taste her full lips and see them wrapped round his dick. Better yet, he'd love to be pumping his cock in and out of her sweet ass while his brother claimed her hot cunt. He had no doubt that she would turn their world upside down the first time they got inside of her.

She had the ample curves they craved on a woman with heavy breasts, a gently rounded belly, and a double handful of ass, plump and begging to be spanked. The thought of his handprint reddening her butt cheeks caused his cock to press harder against the zipper of his jeans. The imprint left there would be painful for hours to come.

"Think she would go with us to the Tidwells' barbeque next weekend?"

Paul had almost forgotten his brother was in the truck with him. His thoughts had been so intent on Lana that it hadn't even registered with him that they were nearly home. Losing his focus wasn't good. He glanced over at his brother and took in the knowing look.

"She's got me in knots, too, big brother." Justin chuckled.

"We can't afford to lose our composure, Justin. Something isn't right about that guy trying to pick her up."

His brother sobered instantly before his eyes.

"Maybe I should call Tidwell now and alert him since the guy didn't have plates on his car."

"It will wait 'til morning. There's nothing he can do tonight anyway. I would almost bet that guy is long gone by now." Paul turned onto their drive.

They lived in a four-bedroom, ranch-style home about ten miles outside of town. Their nearest neighbor was a good five miles away as the crow flies. He liked the solitude and thrived in the wide-open space. He and Justin had renovated the place to suit their tastes in the hopes that one day they would find a woman to share as their wife. Maybe they had found her now. Only time would tell.

Paul cut the engine and started to climb out of the truck when Justin's words stopped him.

"She's the one, Paul. My head is already twisted around her."

He continued out of the truck and walked toward the kitchen door. No way was he going to say anything to that. One of them had to keep their head on straight. The back of his neck tingled, and that always signaled trouble. With Justin already fully involved, it fell to Paul to keep things on an even keel and be ready for whatever happened.

They stepped inside the house, and Justin disarmed the security system before closing and locking the door behind him. Then he set the system to *home* and headed for the fridge. Paul watched him pull out a couple of beers and toss one to him.

"Paul, I'm ready to claim her. I don't want to wait around any longer. It's been long enough, and I'm tired of watching her work herself to death."

Paul sighed and turned up his beer. "We take it slow. I don't want to overwhelm her. She's been here long enough to understand when we tell her we want to date her, but it doesn't mean she's ever considered dating more than one man herself."

"I agree. I just want it out in the open now. I'm tired of acting like a damn stalker checking up on her."

He watched his brother pace back and forth in front of the refrigerator. It hadn't occurred to him that what they had been doing by keeping an eye on Lana was bothering Justin. Maybe it should have. His brother wasn't one for deceit or subterfuge, where he'd once been Special Forces and lived that way for eight years.

Shaking his head, Paul emptied his beer then tossed it in the garbage. "I'm sorry, Justin. I guess I didn't realize it bothered you so much."

"Yeah, well. I understood the need for it at the time, but that time has passed. Her mom's been gone nearly six months now, and she's still working herself to death."

"We'll talk to her, tell her what we want. First we see about her car in the morning and talk to the sheriff."

Justin nodded his head and ran a hand over his face. "I'm going to hit the shower and get some sleep. It's already nearly two."

Paul watched his brother walk out of the room. He should do the same thing. The weather report had promised another scorcher of a day tomorrow. It wouldn't do to be tired on top of hot.

He set up the coffeepot for in the morning and hurried to get in on some of the hot water before Justin used it all. They had a separate hot water heater for the master suite, but that was reserved for when they claimed their wife. Hopefully it would be getting some use real soon.

* * * *

Lana crawled out of bed the next morning much earlier than she had planned. Between the worry over her car and her overactive hormones because of Paul and Justin, she hadn't gotten much sleep. Instead, her dreams had been filled with all sorts of sensual delights centered around the two hunky men, leaving her needy and feeling empty when she woke up.

She stumbled into the bathroom and quickly dressed for the day. In shorts and a T-shirt, she stepped out into the already-warm day to walk back to work to check on her car. To her amazement, it was sitting in her usual parking spot with a note under the windshield wiper.

She quickly grabbed it and hurried back into the apartment. Thinking that Rick had taken care of it and hoping he didn't expect anything personal for the good deed, she laid the note on the kitchen counter and poured a much-needed second cup of coffee. Picking up the piece of paper, she unfolded it and read.

The battery cable was loose. We tightened it and checked it out for you. It shouldn't give you any trouble again. It was signed *Paul and Justin.*

How had they been able to get in it, much less start it without her keys? Lana puzzled over that for several minutes as she sipped her coffee. They probably had no trouble getting into it. It was an old car. Maybe they had hotwired it to drive it over. She shook her head and set her cup on the counter. She needed to start on her housework and make a run to town for groceries before time to go to work. Should she call and thank them or leave it alone? She didn't want to be rude. She decided to think about it for a while.

For the next two hours, Lana washed clothes and cleaned the apartment. She decided to grab a late lunch at the diner and then finish up at the grocery store. By the time she pulled into the parking lot of the restaurant, very few people were left. She'd missed the crowd.

Martha greeted her at the door and waved her over to a booth by the windows.

"What can I get you, Lana?"

"Just a hamburger and a Diet Coke is fine."

"I'll have it right out."

Lana watched Martha lean over the window dividing the front from the kitchen and confer with one of her husbands. She couldn't tell which one it was from where she sat. Martha had two men to look after her. She couldn't say she was used to the practice in Riverbend, but she had been there long enough to have gotten past the initial shock and unease about it.

When her mom had moved there while she had been in college, she hadn't paid much attention to the town. He mom loved it there and had decided on it because one of her best friends from college lived there with her two husbands. It hadn't bothered her mom one bit, and Lana could honestly say that living there had probably helped her mom more than anything during those last years. Everyone had been so nice and helpful.

When her mom passed away, it had never occurred to her to move away. Even though she hadn't been able to keep the house because of the medical bills, she still considered Riverbend her home.

"Here you go, sweetie. One Diet Coke. Your burger will be ready in no time. How are you doing?"

"Fine. Thanks for asking. With school out, it's a little less busy right now."

"I sure hate that you're working at The Burger Hop, though. I wish there had been an opening when you needed it."

"It's no problem. I don't mind working with the teenagers. Keeps me young."

Martha rolled her eyes at her. "Lana, you're so far away from being old you might never get there."

Someone came in the door so Martha hurried away to seat them and take their order. It gave Lana the breathing room she needed. Martha could be a bit overwhelming in her own way. She mothered everyone like they were her children.

Several minutes later, she returned with Lana's meal but hurried off to see about another table. The burger was delicious as usual. She finished it and her Diet Coke before Martha got a chance to return to chat. After leaving a tip, she paid for her meal at the register and waved at the two men in the back as she left.

She spent a little less than an hour in the grocery store because they had moved the aisles around again and she couldn't find anything. Frustrated and tired, Lana hurried back home and unloaded her groceries. She still had to finish up the laundry before time to go to work. She dreaded the coming evening, but she needed the money, and she would be off the next day.

She had just changed into her jeans and The Burger Hop polo shirt when someone knocked on her door. Who could it be? She never had company. Lana checked the peephole and recognized Justin's face. Well, she needed to thank him and his brother for taking care of her car, so this was as good a time as any. Opening the door, she smiled.

"Hi, Justin. Thank you so much for taking care of my car this morning. You and your brother didn't have to do that."

He leaned against the door facing and smiled. "It was our pleasure. Lucky for you it was just a loose battery cable." Then he frowned. "You're going back to work tonight?"

"Um, yeah. I work 'til close. I'm just about to leave now." She hoped he would take the hint and leave, but it didn't look like he had any intentions of doing that.

"I don't like for you to drive back to your apartment that late at night by yourself."

"Well, since it's none of your business, it shouldn't bother you. Be sure and tell your brother that I appreciate the help with the car." She lifted her eyebrows, hoping he would go.

"We talked to the sheriff about the man who tried to get you to get in his car last night. He's looking into it. Strangers driving around Riverbend that late at night are obviously out to cause trouble."

"I'll be extra careful. With my car fixed, I shouldn't have any more problems." She sighed and put her hand on her hip. "Look, Justin, I've got to go or I'll be late."

"I'll wait on you to get your things and walk you to your car."

Realizing he wasn't going to leave as long as she was still there, Lana turned and grabbed her purse and car keys. Then she locked the apartment behind her and led her self-appointed guard toward her car. When she got in he held the door while she fastened her seat belt. Then he leaned in with a smile.

"I'll check on you when it's time to go home. You're not leaving that place alone again." He closed the car door before she could tell him otherwise.

Fuming, she started the car and backed out of her parking place, scowling at him the entire time. He just smiled and waved her off. She watched him climb into his truck in her rearview mirror as she drove off. The nerve of the man telling her she wasn't going to do something. He had no right to tell her what to do. She was nothing to him.

When she clocked in, Rick was waiting on her. He had an unreadable expression on his face when he called her into the office and shut the door behind them.

"Is something wrong, Rick?"

"Your car was still in the parking lot last night when I left. How did you get home?"

"I caught a ride." She struggled to keep her expression normal.

"Why didn't you come get me so I could check it for you? It was probably just your battery. I could have saved you the hassle of having to call a tow truck." She could see barely suppressed anger in his eyes.

Lana wondered if he had deliberately messed with her car so she would have to ask him for help. She quickly dismissed that idea. Rick wouldn't stoop to something that low, would he? She frowned. Then how had he known it was probably her battery? *Lucky guess.*

"I didn't want to bother you. I already had a ride, and they checked the car and brought it to me this morning, so there really wasn't any problem."

"Who did you get to help you?"

"Look, it's really none of your business, Rick. Can I get to work now? I know Tracy is ready to turn the window over to me."

Rick looked as if he wanted to say something more, but he gritted his teeth and nodded his head. Lana hurried out of the tiny office, relieved to be able to draw in a deep breath of fresh air. He had made her nervous with his questions and the angry look in his eyes. What was she going to do if he started bothering her for real? She needed this job. Jobs that would work around her full-time position at the school were hard to come by.

"Sorry, Tracy. Rick had a question about last night." She quickly traded spots with the teenager and counted her drawer as Tracy ran the register report.

"It's been fairly quiet for a Saturday afternoon. Mostly drink orders with it being so hot."

"Let's hope it stays that way. I could use a break." She grinned at the girl as she gathered her things and headed to the back.

As it turned out, the early evening dragged by. She kept busy by cleaning the area and stocking the cups and lids. Around seven that night, Rick walked up and waited for her to hand a drink and an order of fries through the window before interrupting her.

"I'll handle the window for a few minutes. Take a break. Sheriff Tidwell is out front and wants to talk to you. Is something going on, Lana?"

She frowned. "No, nothing that I know of." She handed him her headset and hurried out front.

Just as she got to the door that led out into the lobby, it dawned on her that the sheriff probably just wanted to talk to her about the stranger that had offered her a ride. Relief washed over her, but when she opened the door with a smile, the dark look on the man's face had her smile melting quickly. Something was wrong, and she didn't think she was going to like it.

Chapter Three

"Ms. Peters? I'm Sheriff Mac Tidwell. I don't believe we've ever met before."

Lana shook her head and took the hand he held out. Mac was totally bald and very imposing. She'd seen him around town, of course, but had never had a reason to meet him before. She wished she didn't have to meet him now.

"Um, is this about the car from last night?"

"Yes, it is. Let's go over there where there isn't anyone so we can talk. I won't take up much of your time."

He waited for her to sit in the booth before sliding in on the opposite side. His piercing eyes had her swallowing around a rather hard knot stuck in her throat.

"Justin and Paul told me what happened last night after you left work. Why don't you tell me exactly what happened from when you walked out the door until you got in the truck with Paul and Justin?"

"O–Okay. I walked out with Joseph, who works the grill in the back at night. He waited until I got in my car before he took off in his truck. I never thought that my car wouldn't start."

"So you've never had trouble with it before?"

"Nothing like that. I mean, I've had a flat tire before, but it's always started for me."

"Go on. What happened next?"

Lana nodded and hurried on. "I tried it a couple of times and then got out and locked the door. I thought about getting Rick, but I really didn't want to bother him. I figured it wasn't that far to my apartment, so I could walk."

"Paul said Rick's been bothering you." He seemed to be watching her closely.

"Oh, no. I mean, he's asked me out a few times, but that's really it. I just didn't want to, um, make things worse. You know?" She really felt awkward now. Lana didn't want to cause Rick any trouble.

"So you decided to walk home, at one in the morning—alone."

When he put it that way, it did sound dumb. She looked down at where her hands were clasped tightly in her lap.

"Lana?"

"Um, I got about halfway there when a car pulled up beside me and offered me a ride. He even knew my name. I told him I was almost home, and he said that I still had a long way to go so get in. It bothered me that he seemed to know where I lived."

"What happened then?"

She told him the rest of it and hoped that would be the end of their conversation. Thinking back over the events from the previous night made her nervous again.

"What color was the car? Did you see the driver well enough to describe him?"

"The car was a dark color. Either navy blue or black, and it was a four-door sedan of some kind. I didn't see the man. It was too dark."

The sheriff asked her several more questions about what he sounded like and if she got the feeling that she knew him or not. Lana answered as honestly as she could. When he finished writing down what she had told him, he leaned back against the back of the booth and sighed.

"Lana. There was a woman killed early this morning not far from where you live."

Lana gasped. The sheriff continued.

"She had gotten home late from spending time with her, um, boyfriend and never made it inside her trailer. I don't want you outside at night by yourself anymore. I'm going to talk to Rick about making sure that anyone who works the night shift has an escort home."

"I–I guess Rick will probably follow me when I close at night."

"I don't think you have to worry about that. Paul and Justin both said they plan to see that you get home safely." His mouth twitched as if he were trying to hold back a smile.

"Is that everything, Sheriff? I need to get back to work."

"That's all. You be careful, Lana. Something tells me that you had a close call last night. It's a good thing Paul and Justin drove by when they did." He stood up as she did and followed her back to the counter.

"I'll tell Rick you want to see him." She quickly walked through the door and made her way back to the window.

Rick looked up with a question in his eyes. Did he look a little worried? Lana wasn't sure why she thought that.

"The sheriff wants to talk to you."

He nodded and handed over the headset to her before walking toward the front counter. She had to stop and take a deep breath before she could answer the drive-thru. The idea that someone had gotten murdered not long after she made it home had her insides crawling. As much as she didn't want to get involved with Paul or Justin, she wasn't going to say no to their offer to see her home safely at night.

By the time she had finished cleaning up her area after closing, she was once again exhausted and a nervous wreck thinking about the drive home. She hadn't heard from either Paul or Justin, so she wasn't sure if they still planned to see her home or not. She really didn't want Rick to follow her home.

"Your ride's here, Lana." Rick's sarcastic voice startled her as she was pulling her purse out of her locker.

"Um, thanks, Rick." She turned around and ran right into him.

"I could have followed you home, Lana. You don't need those two sniffing around you. They're depraved, and they're going to want to use you. Once they've had you, they'll drop you and move on to the next easy target."

"I don't know what you're talking about." She moved to walk past him, but he stepped to the side, blocking her path.

"They share their women, Lana. Half this freaking town is like that. It's sick. If you let them, they'll turn you into a whore."

"Stop it, Rick. I'm not seeing them. They're just being nice and making sure I get home safe. Besides, what they do is none of my or your business." This time she managed to squeeze past him. "Are you going to lock the door behind me?"

Lana didn't stop or turn around to be sure he was coming. Right then she didn't care. All she wanted to do was get away from him. She had no idea where Paul and Justin would be, but she hoped they were in the back. She didn't relish walking around the building alone in the dark. When she opened the door, Paul stood there waiting on her.

"You ready?"

At her nod, he held out his hand and gripped her elbow lightly as he ushered her toward her car. Their truck was parked next to it, and Justin was sitting in the driver's seat. When he saw her, he smiled.

"Hi, Lana. How are you doing?"

"Hi, Justin. I'm doing okay."

"You look worn out. We'll get you home in no time."

Paul held out his hand expectantly. She frowned. "What?"

"Give me the keys to your car. I'm driving you. Justin will follow us."

"I can drive my own car, Paul. You don't have to."

"Give me the keys, Lana. I'm driving."

She sighed and handed over her keys. He helped her in the car then got in the driver's seat and started the car. It turned over the first time. He didn't look at her as he pulled out of the parking lot, heading to her apartment.

Lana didn't say anything on the short ride there. She was tired and more than a little unnerved at the turn of events. When Paul pulled into her parking spot, she started to get out, but he stopped her with a hand to her arm.

"What?"

"Wait for Justin to get there to unlock your door."

A soft tap at her window had her jumping. It was only Justin. She unlocked the door and let him help her out. Both men followed her to her apartment. She felt silly now.

"I don't think anything is going to happen to me with you two here. I can walk to my apartment by myself."

"We're not taking any chances where you're concerned." Paul reached out and ran his thumb lightly over her lower lip. "Go on in and lock the door."

She looked from him to Justin and back again. They seemed to be taking everything way too seriously for just being friendly. Maybe Rick was right and they wanted her as a playmate. Her pussy creamed in her panties at the thought. That was not a good sign. She had no intention of being anything to them, much less a playmate.

She unlocked her door and stepped inside. When she turned to close the door, she gave them a shaky smile.

"Thanks for seeing me home, guys. I appreciate it."

"Do you work tomorrow?" Justin asked.

"No. I'm off tomorrow."

"Good. You need to rest. You've got circles under your eyes."

She frowned at him. "Are you saying I look bad?"

"No! I didn't mean it that way. Just that you need some rest." Justin's eyes grew wide.

"We'll talk to you about your schedule for next week later, Lana. Lock up." Paul's eyes held hers for a split second before she blinked and pulled away.

She closed the door and quickly locked it, sliding the dead bolt home before she checked the window to watch them leave. Her mouth watered at the sight of their tight asses walking away. She was in so much trouble.

* * * *

Sunday afternoon, Lana grabbed her Kindle and a Diet Coke with the intentions of going to the park for a couple of hours. She was restless and needed some fresh air and wide-open spaces. Being cooped up working all the time didn't agree with her. It was supposed to be a little cooler with a light breeze for a change. She planned to take advantage of the situation and catch up on her reading in the process.

Before she could open the door, someone knocked. Lana froze for a split second, wondering who it could be. She peeked through the peephole, and once again, Justin's face appeared on the other side of the door. She rested her forehead against the door and closed her eyes, but another loud knock jarred her, and she quickly stood back up to unlock the door and open it.

"What are you doing here?"

"That's not a very friendly greeting, sweetheart." His wide grin only added to her unease.

"I was just going out. What did you want?"

Paul appeared next to him with a frown marring his face. "Where are you going?"

"I don't see where it's any of your business, but I'm going to the park to read and relax for a while."

"See, that's perfect. We're here to take you there." Justin's smile was enticing.

"Why are you taking me to the park?" She was sure her confusion was written all over her face.

"Because you need some fresh air and the park is a nice open public place for us to get to know each other better." Paul's eyes sparkled with amusement.

"But I don't need you to take me. I can go by myself. And why do you want to get to know me?"

"Why does any man want to get to know a beautiful woman? You intrigue us. All we can think about is your delicious body, how your eyes dance when you're angry."

Justin reached out and took her elbow lightly in his hand. "Let's quit wasting time. All the best spots are going to be taken by the time we get there if we don't hurry."

Lana wasn't sure why she allowed them to maneuver her into their truck, but she was going with them for good or bad. Being sandwiched between the two sexy men kept her nerves on edge and her pussy wet. She had never reacted to another man, much less two men, like this. In fact, until recently, she hadn't thought she could actually get riled up during sex. Now she wasn't so sure that she couldn't. Not if her constantly wet panties around these guys was any indication.

They pulled into a parking space near the park, and Justin helped her step down out of the truck. The slight breeze ruffled her bangs and softened the sun's heat as they headed toward an empty spot under a large tree. Before she could plop down on the drought-damaged grass, Justin produced a blanket and spread it on the ground. She realized then that Paul was carrying a cooler and Justin a small box.

"What's in the box?"

Justin grinned. "You'll see soon enough."

She watched him set the box on the ground next to the blanket. Both he and Paul held out their hands. Lana chewed on her lower lip for a second before taking their hands and allowing them to draw her onto the blanket. After helping her to sit down, Justin handed her Kindle to her before removing her sandals. He caressed her ankles then briefly massaged her feet. The sensation left her feeling a bit shaky.

Paul opened a Diet Coke and passed it to her. She took a sip while watching the two men get comfortable on the blanket. They leaned back on their elbows and seemed to watch the Frisbee game several kids were playing. She finally relaxed against the tree and turned on her Kindle to read.

It took her several minutes to lose herself in the book with the two handsome men lounging on either side of her. She couldn't help being aware of them. Paul's smoky scent reminded her of a winter's night sitting in front of a fire. It curled around her and stoked the embers slowly awakening deep within her.

Justin's scent was subtly different. Fresh pine and earthy woods surrounded him. It roused her need for something more, only she wasn't sure what it was. Both men smelled like home to her, and she didn't know what to make of that. Until a few months ago, she had never even heard of them before. Now she was equating them with something serious to her. It had her reading over the same passage several times before she finally managed to settle.

She wasn't sure how long had passed, but Justin sat up and pulled something out of the box he had brought. She pretended to ignore him until Paul joined him and they passed a bottle between them. Curious, she looked up and found both men staring at her, unreadable expressions on their faces that swiftly turned to amusement.

"Time to put some sunscreen on you. You've had enough sun for the day." Justin began smoothing the lotion over her foot and up her leg in soft swirling motions. Paul soon followed suit on the other leg.

"Um, guys. I can do that. Besides, I already put some on before I left the apartment."

"We know. We can smell it—among other things."

It was the "other things" that stopped her from saying more. What more could they smell? The idea that they could smell her arousal mortified her. She couldn't stop wiggling when they reached the hem of her shorts at the top of her thighs.

"Settle down, babe." Paul started rubbing lotion into her arm, moving slowly up to her shoulder while Justin took the other arm.

They continued their sensual massage around the back of her neck and then across her chest above the neck of her V-neck shirt. By the time they had finished, she was one mass of aroused flesh, complete with panting and a dry mouth. She couldn't miss the desire shining from their eyes. Paul's hazel ones sparked, dark and daring. Justin's promised pleasure beyond anything she could imagine, and she could imagine a lot.

Paul slowly lowered his head toward hers. His lips brushed lightly against hers. Then he leaned toward her ear, and his hot breath sent chills down her spine as he spoke.

"Your hot pussy is weeping for us, isn't it, Lana? I can smell your ripe perfume from here."

She could feel the heat seep up her neck and into her cheeks. No one had ever talked that way to her before. It both shocked her and turned her on, sending another rush of liquid heat to her pussy. She struggled to move away, but she had nowhere to go. Justin had crowded in on her other side. He leaned down and licked the outer shell of her ear.

"We're going to love you, Lana, like you've never been loved before."

Their blunt words and promises had jumping beans bouncing around on trampolines inside her stomach. Trapped between them as she was, Lana could only whimper when Paul laid openmouthed kisses along her neck. Each one seared her skin hotter than the last.

"You belong to us, Lana." Paul's words stilled her heart for a split second.

Rick's claims from the night before ran through her mind once again. It was enough to jumpstart her heart. She wasn't one of their women to be used and tossed away when they were through with her. She couldn't deny that she felt something for them, but she wanted more than what they would ever offer her. Lana knew better than to hope for more from them. She swallowed hard and pulled away from them.

"No! No one owns me."

Chapter Four

Justin's heart nearly stopped at Lana's emphatic *no*. Her eyes flashed fire as she scooted up on the blanket and struggled to stand. He quickly steadied her before getting up as well. He noticed Paul's dark expression and shook his head at his brother. They didn't need to push her right now. The stakes were too high with a killer in the area.

"Sweetheart…"

"Don't call me that. I'm not your sweetheart. What is going on? I just met you the other night." She looked from one to the other of them with confusion clouding her eyes.

"We like you, Lana. We want to get to know you." Justin sighed.

"Getting to know me is a far different matter than belonging to you." She crossed her arms and glared at Paul.

Justin shot his brother an exasperated look before schooling his features to try and placate Lana.

"Paul's impatient. We've known that we wanted you since the first time we saw you hanging out at that drive-thru window four months ago. It's been hard waiting to introduce ourselves."

"Why did you wait?"

Paul spoke up this time. "Because we were in the middle of a rush project that took all of our spare time to finish. We didn't want to introduce ourselves and then not see you again for weeks."

"We wanted time to court you like you deserve," Justin added.

"Then what's with the full-court press all of a sudden?" She looked genuinely confused.

"You could be in danger with a killer out there. We want to protect you, and the only way to do that is to spend more time with you. That means speeding up our time line some."

"I don't need you to protect me. I can take care of myself."

Justin quickly placed a hand on Paul's arm. He knew his brother would say something that would only make things worse. He looked into his brother's eyes and saw the pain before he masked it. Paul wasn't the kind of man to show weakness, not even to his brother, so the fact that he'd seen it at all told him just how much Lana meant to him.

"You've been taking care of yourself for too long now. Let us help you. You shouldn't have to struggle so much when we want to make things easier on you."

"Why me? I'm nobody. I'm not beautiful or witty or any of the things that men go for."

"Don't say that about yourself." Paul stepped closer to her. "You're gorgeous and smart. If you don't think men want you, then you're blind. I don't want to hear that crap out of you again."

"Look, I'm not, um, really very good with sex. You will only be disappointed if this goes any further."

Justin wanted to kiss away the self-conscious expression on Lana's face. It was obvious that she didn't have a lot of self-esteem when it came to her body. He couldn't help but wonder why. No one knew much about her other than she had moved home to take care of her mother when she was diagnosed with cancer. What had her life been like before that? He wanted to know everything about her.

"Look. I know I came on a little strong, Lana, but I'm not used to beating around the bush. I want you. *We* want you. While there's a crazed killer running around we're going to be watching out for you, so you might as well get used to it." Paul's stiffened jaw said that he meant business.

Justin waited to see what Lana would do with his brother's declaration of intent. Either he'd succeeded in scaring her off, or she would step up to the challenge. He desperately hoped she wouldn't pull away. It would make keeping her safe that much harder because there was no way he would stop watching out for her.

"Sometimes you don't always get what you want, Paul."

"And sometimes I do."

They were staring at each other as if trying to read the other's soul. Justin didn't move, didn't make a sound as they fought a silent battle between them. Finally, Lana looked away and hugged herself as if she was cold.

"Come on, sweetheart, and have a seat. I've got a cold Diet Coke in the cooler with your name on it." Justin gently took her hand and pulled her back onto the blanket.

As she knelt beside him, Paul pulled the drink out of the cooler and wiped it off before handing it to her. Justin reached inside the box he'd brought and pulled out wrapped-up sandwiches and bags of potato chips.

"Figured the sun would make you hungry."

She gave a half smile and shook her head. "I'm really not very hungry."

The growling of her stomach had both him and his brother chuckling. He enjoyed watching the faint blush stain her cheeks.

"I guess I could maybe eat something," she muttered.

Justin hid his grin and handed her a sandwich and a bag of chips. They ate in a surprisingly comfortable silence despite their earlier argument. He felt sure they could work things out if she wouldn't immediately take things the wrong way and Paul wouldn't act so aggressive.

It always fell on his shoulders to be the peacemaker in their relationships, whether personal or business. He didn't mind for the most part, but sometimes, he wanted the luxury of getting angry about something and expressing how he felt. Now wasn't the time to press it, though. Lana might be in danger, and he wouldn't risk her life for anything.

"Do you like working at the school?" Paul's question came out of the blue.

She smiled and nodded. "I enjoy keeping things running smoothly. I wish I could use more of my business management studies, but for now it's a good job."

"So you majored in business management?" Justin wanted to keep her talking about herself.

"Actually I have a double major, one in that and one in marketing. I had planned to get a job in Dallas or Houston someday."

Justin's eyes met Paul's. It was perfect. They needed a manager for their company who could direct and promote the business while they handled the office work. They would have to use caution, though, in getting her to come to work for them. She would balk at the direct offer of a job, believing that they had manufactured it to get her closer to them. Even if they had, it wouldn't matter. She was all that mattered.

"I really should be getting home now, guys. I've got work tomorrow." She began gathering up the wrappers from the sandwiches and stuffing them in the empty chip bags.

Justin helped her, and they stuffed everything back in his box. Paul folded the blanket with her help then picked up the cooler and the three of them walked back toward the truck. He hoped that everything had smoothed out so there wouldn't be any problem with them coming around more often.

Once they had reached the truck, Justin helped Lana into the cab then swung up next to her. Paul drove them back to her apartment. They all got out despite her frown. When they reached her apartment, Paul took her key from her and unlocked the door before giving back her key. She gave him a small smile. It was a start.

"Thanks for taking me to the park and for the picnic."

"We need to talk about when you're working at night again." Paul placed a hand on the door when she started to close it.

She stared at him for a few seconds but finally sighed and backed into the room, holding the door open wide. They walked in and waited while she walked over to the small kitchen area and pulled a piece of paper off the fridge.

"I work tomorrow night, and Wednesday, Thursday, and Friday nights this week."

"Do you work at all this weekend?" Paul asked.

"Um, no. I'm off Saturday and Sunday."

"Good. We're going to a party Saturday afternoon."

Justin rolled his eyes at his brother's method of asking for a date. Evidently Lana was getting used to his directness because she smiled and shook her head.

"I guess that means you're asking me to go with you."

Paul's lips twitched, obviously trying to keep from smiling. It was the first crack in his brother's armor. He hoped it would be the first of many.

* * * *

Lana couldn't believe that she was flirting with Paul now after his comment from earlier. What was wrong with her? She placed her schedule back on the fridge and walked over to the door in hopes that they would take the hint. She really needed them to leave so she could regain her composure. Being around them was keeping her on edge.

"It's a barbeque and pool party, Lana. It will be fun." Justin seemed eager that she want to attend with them.

"It's going to be at the Tidwells'. You'll enjoy yourself." Paul reached out and fingered a strand of hair that had escaped her ponytail.

She sighed, giving in to Justin's pleading look and maybe to Paul's attempt at acting like he wasn't pleading. It suddenly occurred to her that he demanded things because he didn't expect for anyone to give in to him if he merely asked.

"Okay. What time do I need to be ready?"

"We'll pick you up about two. Wear a bathing suit under your clothes." Justin grinned.

"We'll be waiting on you tomorrow night when you get off at The Burger Hop." Paul's eyes bored into hers.

She was sure he expected her to balk, but she decided that having an escort home wasn't really that bad of an idea right now. She wasn't going to cut off her nose to spite her face. She valued her life even if it did suck sometimes. Right now it didn't suck all that much. She couldn't stop the smile from forming on her face as she looked up at Paul. His eyes registered surprise then suspicion.

"I'm not sure what time I'll get off on a Monday night. We aren't usually that busy, so sometimes I get to go home early."

"Where is your cell phone?" Paul held out his hand.

She frowned but dug in her purse and pulled out her phone. Handing it to him, she watched as he messed with it for a few seconds then handed it back to her.

"I programmed mine and Justin's phone numbers in it for you. Call us if you get to leave early."

"Sure. That way you don't have to come out there if you don't need to."

"No, call us before you leave so we can come on and see you home. I don't care how early it is. We don't want you out alone."

She started to argue but caught a pleading glimpse from Justin and decided to back off. It actually felt good for someone to worry about her for a change. She had never really had anyone do that for her. She had been independent almost from the time that she started school as a six-year-old. Her mom had pretty much left her on her own, though she had always shown her plenty of love. She was just so caught up in trying to make a living that she didn't always have the time or the energy to do more than that. Lana had been proud to be able to take care of herself. At some point, her mom had begun to depend on her more and more as she had grown up.

Now, looking back, she realized that, except for when she'd been seriously ill at fifteen, her mom had depended on her to take care of herself. She never questioned her choices or criticized her decisions. When her mom had moved to Riverbend while she was in college, Lana had looked at it as her mom's way of backing away from depending on her as much. Lana had been happy, believing that she would find a dream job in a big city after school.

Unfortunately, not long after she had graduated college, her mom had been diagnosed with cancer. She had moved to Riverbend to take care of her and spend as much time as possible with her before she was gone. Now she was alone, and the idea of someone worrying over her actually sounded nice for a change.

"Okay. I'll call you as soon as I know."

"What time do you go to work in the mornings?" Justin's voice startled her. She'd been so absorbed with Paul that she'd nearly forgotten about him.

"Um, I go in at eight."

"Good. Plenty of daylight then. You still need to be aware of everything around you, though."

"I will. I'm not taking any chances." She looked at both of them. "Thank you for watching out for me."

"That's what friends do, Lana. They take care of each other. We plan to take real good care of you, babe." Paul's voice dipped lower with the last sentence.

"We'll let you get ready for work tomorrow. Get some sleep, sweetheart." Justin turned and walked over to the door.

Paul followed him, but they didn't immediately open the door. Instead, Paul pulled her into his arms so fast she didn't have time to even squeak. His head lowered toward hers slowly enough that she could have protested, but for some reason, she didn't. Then his mouth touched hers, moving against her lips until she opened for him and his tongue sank in. He held her head between his hands and tilted her head the way he wanted so that he could devour her mouth. His tongue teased and tussled with hers until she could no longer think.

The touch of another set of hands at her waist and the feel of Justin's hard body at her back jerked her back to reality better than a cold glass of water poured over her head. She pushed against Paul. In the process, it moved her closer to Justin. She could feel his erection in the small of her back and stilled.

"Easy, sweetheart." Justin's grip on her waist tightened then he turned her around to face him.

He didn't give her a chance to pull away as Paul had. Instead, Justin took her mouth in a wash of need that sang through his body into hers. His lips devoured hers as his tongue slipped inside to drive her insane with a tenacious aim to make her his. His and Paul's. When he finally pulled back, Lana could barely stand, much less think straight. Her panties were soaked, and her nipples hard pebbles that begged for attention. She realized that while Justin had dominated her thoughts with his kiss, Paul's hands had remained on her as well.

"We'll see you tomorrow night. Don't forget to call us if you can leave early." Paul let go of her and walked through the door.

"Lock up, Lana." Justin snuck in another quick kiss to her cheek before he, too, walked out.

She quickly closed and locked the door before turning and leaning against it, her breath coming in quick pants. What had just happened? Paul's kiss had just about melted her insides. Then Justin's heat at her back had her stomach doing somersaults. And that kiss.

Lana had never felt anything like how she felt around them. When they touched her she couldn't think straight. Paul's kiss had just about turned her inside out while Justin's had pretty much finished the job. Being caught between them, shocks of arousal had flared deep inside her. She couldn't afford to let them get to her. She wasn't strong enough to handle them. They would use her and then move on. She wasn't going to allow that to happen.

Hands shaking, Lana turned and headed straight to the bathroom. She needed a shower, preferably a cold one. Paul and Justin were nice men, but they were out of her league. The sooner she got that through her head, the better off she would be.

Hot prickles of heat helped soothe her frazzled nerves and relax her taut muscles. Lana dressed in clean clothes and began gathering her things for work the next day. After making sure she had her uniform for The Burger Hop hanging by the door so she wouldn't forget it on her way out, it dawned on her that she didn't have a bathing suit for the party the next weekend. Shrugging, she decided to think about it later. If she had time she would try and find one to fit that she could afford. If not, she just wouldn't go swimming.

By nine o'clock, she was tired and ready for bed. Everything was set up for the week ahead, so when she finally settled under the light sheet, Lana was surprised that she had trouble immediately falling asleep. Instead, thoughts of two very handsome men kept circling in her head. Once she finally did drift off, it was no wonder that her dreams included them.

Chapter Five

The week passed quickly for Lana. Between working at the school and her nights at The Burger Hop, she was totally worn out by the time Saturday wound around. She'd been so busy that week that she hadn't had time to locate a cheap bathing suit, so she would have to go without one.

There hadn't been a repeat of the kiss from the previous Sunday, so Lana felt like it had just been a spur-of-the-moment type thing and they hadn't really meant anything by it. She wasn't sure why that disappointed her when she knew she didn't need to get involved with them. She chalked it up to being in a long dry spell for sex and left it at that.

By the time the men showed up at two Saturday afternoon, she had managed to get a little housework done before she showered and dressed for the party. She wore navy-blue Capri pants and a red blouse. She had pulled her hair back into a ponytail and was just stuffing her driver's license and some money in her pocket when she heard knocking at her door.

When she checked the peephole, it proved to be Justin. She quickly unlocked the door and opened it.

"Hi."

"You look great!" Justin's appreciative look did wonders for her self-esteem.

She smiled and grabbed her keys before pulling the door shut behind her. He followed her out to the truck with a guiding hand at her back. After helping her up into the cab to sit next to Paul, he jumped up after her. Both men watched as she fastened the safety belt before Paul pulled out of the parking lot.

"Mac, Mason, and Beth live outside of Riverbend. It's a really pretty place." Justin filled her in on who all would be there.

"Did you and Paul do the landscaping?" she asked.

"Yep. We keep it nice for them. With Mac being the sheriff and Mason handling a busy law career, neither of them have time to deal with it."

"What about Beth?"

Justin chuckled after exchanging a look with Paul. "She's an editor, and there is no way those men would ever let her get her hands dirty outside. They treat her like a princess, like a woman's supposed to be treated."

Lana couldn't imagine a relationship like that at all. She would feel smothered if she couldn't do what she wanted to do. Maybe Beth liked it, though. She started to ask what Beth thought about that, but Justin continued telling her about some of the people who would be there.

"Jared and Quade and their wife, Lexie, will be there. They own a ranch outside of town. I think Lamar, Brody, and Caitlyn will be there as well. They run a machine shop in town. Caitlyn's brother, Brian, his partner, Andy, and their wife, Tish, should be there as well. They own a shop in town."

"I'll never keep all of them straight." The names all started running together in her head.

"You've lived here for several years now, Lana. I can't believe you don't know some of them." Paul glanced her way before returning his attention to the road.

"I spent most of that time with Mom and taking her back and forth to Dallas to her appointments." Not wanting to think about losing her mom, she quickly asked a question about who else would be there.

"I'm not sure if Travis and his brother, Randy, will be there or not. They've been really busy with their ranch lately." Justin named a few other people she didn't know.

By the time they arrived at the Tidwells' place, she was convinced she would be miserable among so many strangers but was determined not to show it. Being nobody with nothing to her name in the midst of that many well-off people didn't help her relax much, either.

When Paul parked behind another truck and climbed out of the cab, Lana stiffened her spine and let Justin help her down and lead her toward the house. It was impressive and had to have at least four bedrooms. The yard around it was meticulously groomed with grass and several trees. There were even flowers in the bed beneath one of the windows.

As they headed around to the back where the sound of music and laughing voices could be heard, Paul took her other hand in his. She couldn't stop the small shiver from the tingles that spread from her hands up both arms from their grips.

A gate was open at the side of the house, and Paul walked through pulling her and Justin behind him. A crowd of about fifteen people milled around the patio and pool area in the back. Three men manned the grill while everyone else was either sitting around one of the tables or swinging their feet in the pool while sitting on the side.

"Hey, Paul, Justin. Come on in and introduce us to that lovely lady." One of the men at the grill walked forward and stuck out his hand.

"Lana, this is Mason Tidwell. His brother, Mac, is the sheriff. I don't see him." Justin squeezed her hand.

"He's inside. He'll be out in a minute." Mason turned to Lana and held out his hand to her. "Hi, Lana. Great to meet you."

"We're going to introduce her around," Justin said.

"Great idea. What can I get you to drink?"

"Beer is fine." Paul turned to her. "What would you like, babe?"

"Um, nothing for me right now. Thanks."

Justin wrapped an arm around her waist and urged her toward one of the tables. She watched as Paul followed Mason over to a cooler near the grill.

"Hey, Justin." A pretty woman with shiny hazel eyes smiled up at them.

"Hi, Beth. This is Lana. She works at the high school. Lana, this is Beth." He pointed toward the other two women sitting at the table. "That's Lexie and Caitlyn."

They all said hi and Beth scooted over on the bench to make room for her. Their smiles all seemed genuine and friendly. She soon found herself immersed in conversation with the three women.

"Where are you from, Lana?" Caitlyn asked her.

"Originally I'm from a little town in east Texas called Redwater. It's near the Arkansas border."

"Are you a teacher at the school?" Beth spoke up this time.

"No. I'm an administrative assistant." She noticed that Lexie kept looking at her with an odd look on her face.

"I know where I've seen you before. You work at The Burger Hop, too." Lexie grinned.

"Um, yeah. I work there part time." She felt her face heat up.

"Goodness, I don't know how you do it. I don't think I could possibly hold up for two jobs. My hat's off to you." Lexie shook her head.

She didn't know what to say, so she didn't say anything. Thankfully, Caitlyn changed the subject.

"Have you girls read the latest Harley James book? It is hot!"

Lexie waved her hand in front of her face as if she were fanning herself. Beth's face actually turned pink. Lana hadn't heard of the author before. She listened as they described some of the scenes in the book. It wasn't long before her face felt hot.

"If you've never read her books, Lana, you've got to get one." Caitlyn grinned. "Do you read erotica?"

"Um, I read romance novels, but I don't think I've ever read anything like what ya'll are talking about."

"Do you have a Kindle?" Beth asked.

She nodded her head, glad that she'd gotten one for herself before her mom died. She'd used it to read to her mom when she wasn't able to rest.

"I'll lend you one from my Kindle. Then if you like it, you can get more. There are a lot of good erotic romance authors out there. Tymber Dalton, Reece Butler, Melody Snow Monroe..."

Caitlyn took up the list. "Jan Bowles, Allyson Young..."

"Whoa, I'll need to make a list." She couldn't help but laugh.

"Honey, once you've started reading them you won't be able to put them down." Lexie giggled.

They continued talking until the men called out that the burgers were ready. Then everyone started fixing their plates. Lana didn't have to look around for Justin or Paul, they came and got her. She hadn't expected that. She thought they would leave her on her own with the other women, but she found that all of the men sought out their wives. They were all very attentive and made sure the women had everything they needed.

Justin and Paul treated her the same way, getting her a Diet Coke and helping her make her hamburger like she wanted it. They even added potato salad and baked beans to her plate for her. All of the attention she received from them had her a little self-conscious. She wasn't used to it.

While she and the other women had been talking earlier, several others had arrived. Justin filled her in, pointing out Silas Atkins and Jace Vincent, Mac's deputies, as well as several others.

"You should recognize them in case you ever need help and we're not around," Paul said.

She didn't say anything, just nodded and continued to eat. She hoped she wouldn't need anyone in law enforcement for any reason. She was surprised that nothing had been said about the recent murder.

It was all the talk at school and The Burger Hop that week. Maybe these ladies didn't gossip like some of the other women did.

"Have you found anyone to help you with your office yet, Paul?" Caitlyn asked.

"Not yet. We need someone good with organization and maybe even some marketing skills to help us promote the business."

"What about you, Lana? You said you had degrees in business and marketing. Wouldn't that be better than working at The Burger Hop?" Lexie asked.

"Oh, well, I'm sure they're looking for someone full time, and I have my job at the school." She was appalled, worried that the guys would think they had to consider her since she was with them.

"We thought about it, but weren't sure we could convince her to leave her job to work for us. It would be perfect for us," Justin said.

"What do you think, Lana? Are you interested?" Paul's deep voice startled her.

"Well, I–I don't know."

"We'll talk more about it later." Justin seemed to understand that she felt trapped.

She was certain that they wouldn't be able to afford to pay her enough to leave her job with the school. Besides, working for them when she was sort of seeing them wasn't a good idea. What happened when they got tired of her? She'd lose her job, she was sure.

Once everyone was finished eating, the women all worked to straighten up and put away the leftover food while the men cleaned up the patio and grill. Then they all began taking off their clothes right out on the patio. Lana's mouth fell open, but she quickly closed it. They were all wearing swimming trunks underneath. She slipped off her shoes and sat on the side of the pool, dipping her feet in the cool water.

"Hey, didn't you wear your suit under your clothes?" Paul asked as he folded his jeans and sat them next to his boots.

She couldn't take her eyes off of his sculpted body. Justin stepped into view, and she had to draw in a deep breath to keep from hyperventilating at the picture they made. Muscular arms and well-defined pectorals gave way to washboard abs and thick thighs. She slowly lifted her eyes back up to rest on Justin's.

"Um, I didn't have one and didn't get time to go shopping."

"Hey, I've got one you can borrow." Beth grabbed her hand and pulled her up. "Come on."

Lana found herself following behind the other woman as she walked inside the beautiful house. The kitchen was ultramodern, and she caught a glimpse of a formal dining room to the right as she walked into the den.

"I've got several, so you should be able to find one that will fit well enough. You're about my size."

"I appreciate it, Beth. I don't mean to be a bother."

"Nonsense. It's no bother. You won't have any fun if you're sitting on the sidelines while the rest of us are in the pool."

Beth laid out several suits in various styles and colors. She quickly chose the only one-piece and slipped it on in the bathroom. It fit her well enough that she didn't think she would be too embarrassed by the way she looked in it. When she walked out of the bathroom, Beth smiled and nodded.

"That's perfect. Come on and let's have some fun."

She grabbed her clothes and hurried behind Beth back outside. Everyone was already in the pool when they made it out. Justin immediately held out his hands for her to jump in. Appalled at the idea of him trying to catch her, she shook her head.

"I'll get in at the ladder."

When she backed down the ladder, it was to find Paul waiting on her. He pulled her back into his arms and walked toward the middle of the pool. At least in the water she wasn't as heavy. Justin joined them and gave her a quick kiss before she knew what he was doing.

"You look delicious in that bathing suit." His gaze grew heated.

Mac and Mason stretched a net across the width of the pool and the women all got on one side with the men on the other. They played pool volleyball for nearly an hour before everyone began to stretch out and lounge around in the late afternoon sun.

Lana found herself on a lounge chair with Paul on one side of her and Justin on the other. They seemed to take great pleasure in applying sunscreen that they had brought with them. She'd put some on before they picked her up, but she was sure it was long gone by now. It gave her a funny feeling that they had thought about her and brought it. Men didn't normally think about things like that.

The touch of their hands on her bare skin felt wonderful at first then it became arousing as they skimmed her breasts and the tops of her thighs near her mound. She was sure the bathing suit was wet from her pussy juices by now. She was glad when they had her turn over so they could do her back. It hid her protruding nipples.

Once they had finished, she remained on her stomach to give her body time to cool off. Who knew she could become so aroused from just their touch? She had about convinced herself that the last Sunday had been a fluke, but now she knew better. They did this to her.

"Lana?" Justin's sexy voice roused her from the comfortable lethargy she'd drifted into.

"Yeah?" She opened her eyes to find him leaning over her so close that she could feel his breath against her face.

"Ready to call it a day?"

She smiled and started to sit up. He stood up and helped her to her feet.

"Let me change clothes."

"Oh, don't worry about it. You can wear it home, and I'll get it another time. It's not like I don't have several to choose from." Beth waved at her.

"Thanks, I'll wash it so it will be clean." Lana quickly pulled on her blouse but didn't bother with the pants. She had her underwear folded up inside them.

"I had a great time, Beth. Thanks for having me and for the use of your bathing suit."

"It was our pleasure. We enjoyed meeting you." Beth, Mac, and Mason saw them out to the truck.

Justin helped her up then slid in next to her. Once Paul had settled in on the driver's side, they all waved and he backed out of the drive and turned them around. Lana couldn't remember another day where she'd enjoyed herself so much. She hated for it to end.

The idea that she might not see them again after this weighed heavily on her heart. She knew she didn't need to get involved with them, but there was something about them that caused her heart to flutter. There were feelings that she hadn't thought she was capable of when they were near.

She closed her eyes, wishing that things were different. She wished that for once she could just enjoy herself without worrying about what would happen next. Unfortunately she was a creature of habit, and it was her habit to worry about consequences and there would be those if she spent any amount of time with the two men. Lana didn't think she was strong enough to survive the aftermath.

Chapter Six

By the time they arrived back at her apartment, Lana was fighting sleep. The lazy afternoon in the sun had zapped all of her strength. Paul put the truck in park and turned off the ignition. Justin chuckled next to her and she wondered what was so funny.

"I think she's asleep."

"Naw, she's awake, but she's fighting it."

"Not asleep." It took all her strength to push the words out of her mouth.

"See." Paul opened his door first.

Justin reached over her and unfastened her seat belt before pulling her toward him. When he lifted her onto his lap, she gasped and jerked awake.

"Hey! I'm awake."

"Sure you are, sweetheart. Let us get you inside." Justin chuckled once again.

He leaned out of the truck and passed her over to Paul. He held her tightly against his chest as Justin got out and led the way to her door.

"Where's your keys, babe?" Paul asked.

"In the pocket of my pants."

"I've got them." Justin was sticking the key into the lock.

Once he had the door unlocked, both men walked into her tiny apartment and Justin closed the door.

"I know you're sleepy, Lana, but you're going to have to lock up after us, so wake up." Paul slowly lowered her feet to the floor and let her slide down his body until she was standing up.

She hadn't been able to ignore the large bulge of his cock as she slipped past it. It felt huge. That alone served to wake her up.

"Um, would you like some coffee before you go home?"

"Sure. Let me help you." Justin followed her into the tiny kitchen.

"That's okay. There's not a lot of room in here. I can manage to make the coffee without help."

Justin seemed to ignore her, because he situated himself inside the little alcove while she set up the pot. She was hyperaware of the two men in her apartment just as she had been all day long. Every touch of their skin against hers set off fireworks inside of her. It was no wonder she was shaking as she tried to pour the water into the coffee maker.

"There, shouldn't be long." She turned from the counter and ran headlong into Justin.

He wrapped his arms around her and pulled her against him. "You smell like soft summer rain."

"It's probably the chlorine from the pool."

She heard Paul chuckle in the other room. Justin stared deep into her eyes for a few seconds before he let her go and pulled her back into her tiny living area.

"Would you be interested in working for us, Lana?" Paul's question came out of nowhere.

"We could really use your help, Lana. Neither one of us is very good at handling the business end of things." Justin continued the offer. "Caitlyn is going to do our taxes and will set up our books for us, but we don't have anyone to take care of it on a day-to-day basis. We don't have time."

"It sounds like you need someone full time, and I already have a full-time job."

"That doesn't pay you enough so you don't have to work two jobs." Paul's voice was harsh.

"It's not bad, but I have my school loans, and I'm still paying some on Mom's hospital bills."

"We can afford to pay what you're worth, sweetheart. " He named a salary that had her blinking.

It was much more than she was making at the school along with her part-time work at The Burger Hop. Surely they were kidding.

"Believe me. You'll work for your salary, Lana. There's a lot to running a business. You'd be responsible for scheduling jobs and the materials for that job as well as handling the marketing for the business."

"I–I don't know what to say."

"Say yes." Justin took her hands in his and squeezed them lightly.

She fought to think beyond the emotions swirling inside of her. Being near them every day would be hell to deal with. She was much too aware of them and attracted to them to be able to mask her feelings for long. They would eventually tire of her unless she could manage to keep everything on a business level.

"I need to think about it. It's a big step for me to change jobs like this."

"Just think about only having one job to deal with every day." Paul reminded her of one of the pluses of taking their offer.

"Um, I think the coffee is ready. Let me get it."

"I've got it." Justin slipped past her into the kitchen. "How do you like your coffee, sweetheart?"

"Black." She couldn't take her eyes from Paul's. They were mesmerizing in their intensity.

Justin returned with three cups of coffee in his big hands. He passed one to her and handed another to Paul. She took a quick sip and nearly scalded her mouth. Paul took a seat on the loveseat, stretching his long legs out in front of him. Justin sat next to him. It left the rocking chair for her. She carefully sat down, wondering how she was going to get through the next few minutes.

"When do you work next week?" Paul set the cup on his knee.

"I work Monday, Wednesday, Saturday, and Sunday."

Paul grunted then frowned. He obviously didn't like her schedule. There was nothing she could do about it. They didn't have to see her home at night. She was perfectly capable of taking care of herself. The memory of the night her car had not started slammed back into her. Well, as long as her car worked she could take care of herself.

"What are your plans for tomorrow?" Justin suddenly asked.

"Um, just some housework." She couldn't think fast enough to come up with anything else to make it sound like she was busy.

"Why not come over to our place and we'll show you the office and what has to be done. That will help you see more of what you'll be doing if you come to work for us."

Lana quickly glanced over at Paul. It didn't look as if he cared one way or the other. She would like to know more about the job. Was she really thinking about taking it?

Lana, you'll end up heartbroken without a job if you do.

"I suppose that would be a good idea."

"Good. We'll pick you up around ten in the morning. We'll make a day of it and show you around our place."

She nodded as they both stood up. Justin took Paul's empty cup and walked over to the kitchen sink. He rinsed the cups and left them in the sink.

"We'd better go and let you get some sleep if we're going to be picking you up in the morning." Paul walked toward the door.

Lana set her cup on the little table by the rocking chair and followed him and Justin to the door. Paul turned at the door and pulled her to him. He bent over her and took her mouth in a kiss so soft and tender she ached from wanting more. It was so unlike the intense man she was used to. When Justin moved in behind her and began nibbling along her shoulder, she moaned into Paul's mouth. The sound seemed to ignite him. He deepened the kiss until she was clinging to him.

His tongue swept into her mouth through her parted lips and plundered her, twisting and turning with hers. He sucked her lower lip in and nipped it before soothing it with a soft lick. Her hands fisted in his shirt as the kiss made her burn for more. Then Justin was turning her toward him and it was Paul's hard body at her back as he ran his hands up and down her arms, whispering naughty suggestions in her ear.

When Justin finished kissing her, she didn't think she could stand up without help. There was no disguising the huge bulges in either man's jeans. When she pulled her eyes away from the tempting treats, Paul's knowing look almost did her in.

"Lock up behind us. We'll pick you up at ten in the morning." He stared down into her eyes one more time before pulling the door open and walking through it.

Justin winked at her and followed behind his brother. Lana had to make herself move to close the door behind them. She slipped the locks into place and walked over to where she'd set her cup and picked it up.

By the time she'd washed up the coffeepot and the cups, she was in a little better control of herself. What had gotten into her? She'd acted like a lovesick teenager. There was no way she could work for them if they had that kind of power over her. They would have her in their bed in no time and then what would happen? No, she couldn't work for them.

As she pulled off her T-shirt and then the borrowed swimming suit, Lana began to relax. Having made the decision not to take their offer, she wondered if she should call them and decline to visit them the next day. She checked the time and noticed that it was pushing midnight. No, she wouldn't do that. She needed to tell them in person that she couldn't take their offer.

It occurred to her once she'd finished her shower that she would be alone with them on their territory tomorrow, and just because she wasn't going to work for them didn't mean she wasn't going to sleep with them. Somehow that didn't worry her nearly as much as it should have.

* * * *

Paul and Justin picked Lana up right on time and drove her out to their home on the opposite side of town from where the Tidwells lived. When they pulled up into their drive, Lana nearly gasped out loud at the lovely two-story home with the wraparound porch. It was much nicer than she had expected and could have popped out of one of her daydreams of what her perfect house would look like.

"I take it by your smile that you like it." Justin's chuckle irritated her.

She frowned at him but quickly turned her attention back to the house. There was a detached garage with a covered walkway to the house itself. As soon as Paul had parked and Justin had helped her down, she strolled through the walkway, admiring the lovely beds of brightly colored flowers and shady landscape.

The walkway led to a door set below the wraparound porch, making her curious about what she would find behind the pale blue door. To her astonishment, Paul unlocked the door and ushered her inside into a large room that was obviously a cellar. A set of stairs led upward toward yet another closed door. This time, Justin stepped up to lead the way. He unlocked the door at the top and Lana found herself inside a brightly lit kitchen complete with a separate washroom and pantry.

The appliances were all stainless steel and looked to be fairly new. It was a large eat-in kitchen with plenty of counter and cabinet space. She could easily see a family living there, eating around the large oak table off to the side.

"It's such a lovely room, all bright and shiny."

"Thanks. We like it. Paul cooks when we're not too busy."

She flashed an astonished glance at the other man. He frowned at her, but she noticed a slight twitch to his mouth as if he couldn't quite stop a smile from forming.

"Well, if I waited on Justin to cook, we'd starve."

She hid her grin at that. Next they led her into an open living area that screamed uber geek with its massive flat-screen TV and amazing sound system built in around it. She could easily imagine that there were several hundred CDs and DVDs lining the many shelves covering that wall. Massive, comfortable lounge chairs sat in front of the TV as well as a couch off to one side and a club chair on the other. She couldn't imagine how they could get any work done with something like this in their house. She would die a happy couch potato with something like that at her disposal.

Just when she thought they were through with the downstairs, Paul surprised her with another section situated off of the living area. It looked like it had once been either the master bedroom or a guest suite.

"This is the office area. It's a mess because we don't have time to deal with it."

He was right about that. The desk sat at one end of the large room with bookshelves and file cabinets lining the surrounding walls. The desk itself was probably a pretty dark oak from what she could see of it, but with all the papers, files, and graph paper, it was difficult to tell for sure. There were file drawers half closed with papers and files sticking out them as well. Even the bookshelves had piles of books and papers in no apparent order.

"There's a bathroom through there." Paul indicated a door to the left.

Lana walked over to the set of French doors at the back of the room and noticed that they opened up to a private deck complete with lounge chairs and a small table. It would be a perfect place to take lunch when the weather cooperated. She looked back over at the desk and winced.

"You weren't kidding when you said you didn't like the office part."

Justin chuckled from the doorway. "Nope. It'll be a challenge for anyone to straighten out our mess. I think that's why we haven't been able to get anyone to work for us."

"I don't know anything about landscaping or gardening."

"What little you would have to understand, we can teach you. I suspect you would pick it up faster than you think." Paul walked closer to where she stood just behind the desk.

"Come on and I'll show you the rest of the house." Justin held out his hand.

Lana walked around the desk and let him usher her out of the room and up a staircase. He pointed out his room and Paul's room. They shared a bathroom between them. Then he showed her the master suite complete with a massive walk-in shower and Jacuzzi. The two walk-in closets had built-in shoe shelves and had plenty of light.

She admired the warm golds of the comforter on the bed and the curtains on the windows. The hardwood floors complemented the lovely oak dresser and dual chests. It was a shame the room wasn't being used. It surprised her that neither of the men had chosen to use it. She almost asked Justin why but decided it was none of her business.

Next, he showed her an empty bedroom that had yet to be painted or set up. It was a little smaller than the other two single rooms, but still a nice size. It also had its own bathroom.

"We'll get to it one day. Right now, we've got all we can handle as it is." She had noticed a sparkle in his eyes when he had showed it to her.

She couldn't help but wonder why he looked so mischievous in that moment. It was almost as if he knew something she didn't, and perhaps he did. She just shook her head and followed him back down the stairs to the living area where Paul had turned on some music.

"What did you think of the rest of the house?" Paul asked as she walked back into the room.

"Impressive. Everything is so nicely decorated. Well, except for the last room. Justin said you hadn't gotten to it yet."

Paul and Justin exchanged glances, but Justin didn't say anything right away. Instead, he walked her over to the couch.

"Have a seat. Would you like something to drink? We've got beer, red wine, tea, and water.

"Tea sounds good. Thanks."

He disappeared back into the kitchen. Justin sat down on one side of her and stretched out with one arm along the back of the couch.

"Do you think you would be interested in the job? We could sure use you."

Paul walked back in with a glass of tea and two beers. Justin reached around her and took one of the beers. She accepted the glass and took a sip before setting the glass on a coaster on the coffee table. She watched Paul sit down next to her and turn up his beer before balancing it on his knee.

"Lana?" Justin prompted.

"It does look like you need some help. It would take several weeks to organize everything, I'm sure. Then what would I be doing after that to keep busy?"

"Between answering the phone and handling the accounts, there would be ordering supplies we need and setting up marketing strategies. We have several accounts where we do all the maintenance of their yards and grounds, but we also do development of new landscapes and ground work. We install irrigation systems and put up fences when needed." Paul looked over at Justin.

"Wow, how do you handle all of that between just the two of you?"

Justin grinned. "We have a small crew of full-time workers and usually hire several part-time workers each summer, which is our busiest time."

"I guess I hadn't realized that you had that large of an operation. Just keeping it all straight has to be a big undertaking."

"Which is why we need you." Justin's fingers began tugging lightly on her hair.

Lana hadn't realized that she'd leaned against the back of the couch at some point. She couldn't help the small shiver that traveled down her spine from Justin's teasing fingers. She hoped he didn't notice how he was affecting her. She knew accepting the job wouldn't be such a good idea. How had she gotten this far without telling them no as she had planned the night before?

God, I'm really thinking about it. Not a good idea, Lana.

"So, do you think you want to take it on?" Paul was leaning forward, holding his beer bottle between his knees.

"It really sounds interesting, and I would enjoy the challenge. Working at the school isn't much of a challenge at all." She nibbled on her lower lip.

Justin's fingers were drawing circles on her shoulder now. The sensation was distracting to say the least. How was she supposed to really think things through while he was touching her? How could she not consider accepting the position? The salary would more than pay her bills, including her student loans and the residual hospital bills. With that kind of money she would eventually be able to move out of the rat trap of an apartment into something nicer and safer.

"What would the hours be?" she finally asked.

"Essentially, that would depend on you. We would definitely want you there by eight each morning. You'd work Monday through Friday. Even though we work a lot of weekends, you wouldn't be required to. Unless something drastic happens, you wouldn't need to travel to any of the job sites, either." Justin continued to add that she would have free reign of the house while she was there, too.

"If you wanted to cook your lunch or just warm something up in the microwave, you're more than welcome to use the kitchen." Paul's skin seemed to radiate warmth where his thigh touched hers on the couch.

Lana was finding it harder and harder to concentrate. All she could think about now was how good they smelled and how much she wanted to feel their lips on her again.

"Lana?" Paul's voice jerked her head toward him.

"I'm sorry. What did you say?"

He chuckled. "I asked if you would have to give much notice at the school before you could start."

"Oh, I'd have to give two weeks' notice for sure."

"So that means if you give your notice tomorrow, you could start by the first of July, then."

"Um, yeah, I guess." She was totally confused now. Had she said yes?

"Great! We'll plan for you to start that Monday. You should be able to go ahead and quit The Burger Hop right away." Justin's excitement showed in his voice.

"I'll have to finish out this schedule. It ends on Sunday."

She could see that Paul didn't like that, but there was nothing he could do about it. She wasn't going to quit like that. She owed Rick for taking a chance on her when she needed a job. Plus, she needed that paycheck to cover the rest of her rent for the next month.

Another thought hit her. With her working for the two men, she would have to stop seeing them outside of work. That realization hurt. She really liked them, especially their kisses. It had been the first time she'd really responded to anyone before. Was the job worth losing that? She sighed. Since she knew they wouldn't have remained interested in her for long anyway, the job was much more important. She could do without sex, but she couldn't do without eating or a roof over her head. Somehow, that thought didn't give her much comfort. Instead, she felt her heart sink, and it took her smile with it.

Chapter Seven

Paul noticed how her face changed from smiling and excited to sad and resigned. What had happened? What was going on in that head of hers? He wasn't going to allow her to have second thoughts.

"Now you will have to look at taking up a hobby with all the free time you'll have on your hands by working for us."

"I hadn't thought about that." Her lips curled up into a small smile once again.

"What do you like to do when you're not working?" Justin spoke up, flashing a questioning look at Paul.

"I like to read. I used to cross-stitch, but I haven't done that in a long time. I really don't have any hobbies. I spent four years studying and working while I was in school, and then I was taking care of Mom, so I don't know what I might like to do."

Paul could think of some things he would like her to do, but they might have to work up to that. Right now, he wanted to kiss her. No, make that *needed* to kiss her. He was dying to taste her again. Before she could react, Paul pulled her back into his arms as he leaned against the couch and slid his mouth over hers. She immediately opened to him, allowing him access to her sweet mouth. He explored the cavern's every nook and cranny as his tongue tangled with hers. Her soft moans drove him to conquer her every secret.

He felt Justin pulling her toward him. Reluctantly, he let her go. She whimpered until Justin captured her lips with his. Then she sank into his brother much as she had relaxed into his embrace. She was perfect for them, responsive and beautiful as well as smart. He would do everything in his power to assure that she became theirs. Even if that meant stepping back some to allow Justin to woo her for them.

Paul knew that he tended to be gruff and short when dealing with people. It was just his personality. Justin had gotten all the smooth moves and social abilities between them. He didn't waste time moaning over it or being jealous. It was just how they were each wired. Instead, he focused on what he was good at and did it well.

His cock grew even harder, if that were possible, just watching how she responded to his brother. Her arms were wrapped around his neck with the fingers of one hand deep in Justin's hair. She was pressing her gorgeous breasts into his chest and making the most arousing little noises as Justin devoured her mouth.

She whimpered as he pulled away, arms still tight around his neck. Then she seemed to come to herself and abruptly let go, attempting to slide off of Justin's lap.

"Easy, Lana. Everything is okay."

"No, it's not. I can't kiss you if I'm going to be working for you. It's not right."

Paul felt a smile ease over his mouth at the panicked note in her voice. Seducing her into their bed was going to be a challenge. There was no doubt of that, but getting her away from that fast-food joint was much more important at the moment. Still, he didn't plan on giving up their pursuit of her. They would just have to be a little more subtle at first.

Seeing Justin's lust-filled eyes, Paul sighed. Maybe that wasn't going to be feasible, though. Neither one of them wanted to wait indefinitely to claim her.

"It's our business, babe. We can make any rule we want to, and not kissing the bosses is definitely not a rule. In fact, we may have to make it a rule that you must kiss the bosses when they demand it." Paul actually grinned at the shocked expression on Lana's face.

"What's going on? Do you or don't you need someone to run the office?"

* * * *

Lana jumped to her feet and faced the couch. She narrowed her eyes at the two men in an attempt to regain control of her emotions once again. They were up to something. She could feel it. Not to mention Paul's last statement about making it a rule that she would have to kiss them if they wanted her to. She took a step back and would have fallen backward over the coffee table she had forgotten about if they hadn't lunged for her and kept her upright.

Once again she had their hands on her, touching her. Her head was spinning with a deluge of feelings and emotions. She didn't know how to process them all at one time. Her body reacted to them as if they had been lovers for years. How was she supposed to fight that?

"Careful, sweetheart. You're going to hurt yourself." Justin held her wrist in one hand while the other hand rested lightly on her abdomen.

Paul held her other arm with both hands. While his grip was strong, it wasn't tight and didn't run the risk of bruising her. Neither man had done anything to harm her since she'd known them. When she lifted her gaze from where their hands were, they both looked at her with smoldering gazes before slowly releasing her arms.

"Sweetheart, we're not going to hide the fact that we're interested in you on a more intimate level. You're beautiful, and there's just something about you that calls to us. It's like you're a magnet and we can't resist your allure."

Lana shook her head back and forth and folded her arms across her belly. "It won't work. We're nothing alike. I come from poor white trash and you're obviously leaders here in Riverbend. What do you want from me? To be your mistress? Well, I won't be your plaything, waiting around for when you've got an itch that needs scratching. I want more from life than to be your office manager with benefits."

"Shh, Lana. You don't know what you're talking about." Paul's attempt to calm her down only riled her up worse.

She quickly slipped around the coffee table and walked toward the kitchen and the back door. She knew it would be a long walk home, but she wasn't going to stick around for them to try and change her mind, because she knew that it wouldn't take much for them to convince her to do almost anything they wanted. Where they were concerned, she was just that weak.

Although Paul was closer to her, Justin reached her first. He grabbed her by the upper arms and jerked her back against his front, leaving no doubt that he was hard as steel and well endowed. It caused her to shiver.

"Hold on just a minute. I think you're jumping to conclusions without all the facts." He swung her around to face him, backing her up against the kitchen door.

"Fact one, we like you—a lot. Fact two, we want to get to know you better. Fact three, you enjoy our company."

When she started to tell them it wasn't true, Justin hurried on.

"Don't try and say that's not true, because your nipples stay poked out and you're always wet when we're around."

"I can't help that my body responds to yours. It doesn't mean anything. You're good-looking guys. Of course I'm going to react, just like you get a hard-on around pretty women. It's just a fact of life."

"Wrong. We don't get erections around just any pretty girl. She has to be special, and you're special, Lana." Paul's voice had gotten deep again.

"Are you telling me that you get all hot and bothered around any good-looking man? Are you saying that your pussy gets wet around Rick?" Justin demanded.

"No!"

"Then don't try and deny that we've got something special going on between us."

"There are two of you! I can't have a relationship with both of you."

Justin grinned. "So that's the problem. You're scared of caring about two men at one time. Are you afraid of what will happen when we make love to you together?"

"I–I haven't really thought about it."

"Now you're lying to us. I can see it in your eyes." Paul moved closer to where Justin had her pinned to the door.

"Please." It came out in a whimper.

"Please, what, Lana?" he asked.

"Please don't do this."

"Do what?" Justin leaned in and ran his tongue against her lower lip.

"Seduce me. I know you can, and there wouldn't be anything I could do to stop you."

"What's wrong with letting us show you how good it could be between us?" Paul stopped a few feet from her, standing to one side as he watched Justin nuzzle her neck.

"You'll just get tired of me in a few weeks or months. Then where will I be without a job?" She hated that they had reduced her to begging.

"No, babe. We'll never get tired of you. Don't you get it? You mean so much more to us than anyone we've ever been with before."

"Give us a chance, sweetheart. Let us show you all the wonderful things you've been missing. We'll take good care of you." Justin kept kissing her neck down to her shoulder.

She couldn't think with him doing that. She knew they weren't going to let her leave without a firm answer. She had no doubt that if she said no or stop, they would. They weren't bullies. The problem was that she didn't want to say no or stop. She wanted them. She wanted to experience what they promised. Just once, she wanted to know what being a woman really felt like. Then, when things were over, she'd pick up and move on.

God, was she really considering it? A little voice inside of her tried to remind her that she wasn't sophisticated or part of the in crowd there in Riverbend. She lived in a crappy, rundown apartment building, and they lived in a huge, four-bedroom mansion out in the country. When that didn't seem to be working, the little voice reminded her that she didn't have the right kind of clothes to be seen with them in public if they even wanted to drag her out with them. So she would be making good money working for them. She could afford to add to her wardrobe if the need arose.

Finally, she realized that Justin had stepped back to stand next to Paul and was no longer touching her. He had moved as if to give her room to think. She looked up at the two men and took in their expressions. Justin's held hope and worry while Paul's was completely blank. He wasn't going to let her see inside of him, but she could imagine that he felt much the same way as his brother.

Lana bit her lower lip once again. Their eyelids lowered just a fraction, and a grunt escaped Justin's mouth. He wasn't immune to her. That made her follow the quick nip of her lip with a sweep of her tongue over the offended tissue. To her amusement, both men sighed.

"If I say yes to this job offer, are you going to micromanage every little thing that I do?"

"Absolutely not." Paul stood up straight. "We wouldn't have offered you the job if we didn't think you had the ability to do it. We'll let you do the job as you see fit as long as it gets the desired effect."

"So that means that you will trust me to handle everything?"

"Once we've shown you the ropes, we'll stand back and let you do your stuff." Justin grinned.

He knew they had won, and she was going to take the job and eventually give in to their demands to let them love her. Whoa, not love. Love played no part in this. It was simply lust, and there was nothing wrong with a little lust. Still, she planned to resist them as long as she could. She was still sure that once the new had worn off of a relationship with her they would eventually tire of her.

"Okay. I'll take the job at the salary you offered. I've got to work out my schedule this week and my notice of two weeks for the school, but I can still work a little bit beginning the week after next to get the ball rolling."

"Excellent! You won't be sorry. I can't wait to get you started in the office." Paul's enthusiasm seemed out of proportion to his usual calm façade.

It surprised her so much that she frowned at him. This just seemed to make him smile even more. Justin pulled her into his arms and swung her around until her feet left the ground.

"Okay, let's fix something for dinner and celebrate." Justin let her down so that her feet reached the floor.

"Oh, well I need to be leaving. I have to get ready for work tomorrow."

"Not to mention that you've got to prepare your resignation letter for the school. I think a simple 'I quit' for Rick should suffice, though." Paul winked at her.

Lana didn't answer him because she had no intentions of just saying that she quit. She would type up a resignation letter for Rick as well. He'd given her a job when she'd been desperate. She owed it to him.

Justin pulled out his keys. "I'll drive." Lana and Paul followed behind him as he hurried out to the truck. Once Paul had locked up the house, he helped her up into the truck and assured that she fastened her safety belt before giving a nod at Justin that they could leave.

Justin kept up a lively conversation the entire trip back to town and her apartment. When they had pulled into the parking lot, Lana tried to tell them that they didn't have to walk her to the door, but they both insisted on it. She had no intentions of inviting them in, but it didn't seem to matter. Paul wrapped his arm around her and pulled her in for a kiss. Justin rested his hands at the swell of her hips and pressed against her from behind.

Lana didn't fight the kiss. Instead, she wrapped her arms around Paul's neck and let him lead her where he wanted to take her. Their tongues dueled before he finally released her and pulled back. He let his brother turn her toward him as he rubbed his hard cock against her lower back, dipping down so that it pressed between her ass cheeks before moving back up once again.

When Justin finally pulled back, her panties were soaked and her lips swollen from their kisses. A soft hum seemed to fill her body with a need that she knew wouldn't be sated by her vibrator alone. She was sure they had done it on purpose so that she would not only think about them all week, but also be primed and ready for when they got ready to push their relationship further. For some reason, Lana couldn't be angry with them. For the first time in her life, she felt truly alive. Nothing was going to stand in the way of that. Not even her nosey good intentions.

Chapter Eight

She was rather surprised that her resignation letter was accepted so easily at the school until the principal called her into the office to talk to her. It seemed they were happy for her because they had been about to let her go. The school district had been under orders to cut costs before the next school year, and her job was considered to be expendable. Paul and Justin's job offer had come in the nick of time for her.

Rick, however, didn't take her resignation as well. When she had handed him her letter, he'd frowned at her and opened it to read it. Then he'd grabbed her by her upper arm and dragged her into his office.

"I thought you needed this job to pay your bills?"

"I did. I really appreciate your giving me the job when I needed it, but now I don't. I'm taking another full-time position that pays enough that I don't need a second job anymore."

"Where? I didn't think anyone was hiring around here."

"I'm going to be working for Paul and Justin for their landscaping business."

Rick's mouth opened then closed again. "You're crazy! They are just trying to get in your pants. Once they've had you, they won't want you anymore, and you'll be without a job at all."

"Gee, thanks, Rick, for having so much confidence in my job skills." She started to open the door to walk out, but he stopped her.

"I've seen how they've looked at you when they are up here. They just want to fuck you, Lana. Don't throw away your reputation by getting mixed up with them."

"Rick, it's really none of your business. While I greatly appreciate the chance you gave me, I won't allow you to talk to me this way. If you can't behave appropriately, I might as well leave now."

"Don't." He ran a hand through his hair. "At least work out the rest of this week since you're on the schedule." Even though he sounded resigned to her decision, she could tell that he was still trying to think of some way to change her mind.

Too bad. It wasn't going to happen. Her job at the school was no longer needed. She and Rick agreed that Friday night would be her last shift. She needed to tell the guys that she was available to start in a week instead of two weeks when they came to pick her up. No doubt they would be happy since they hadn't wanted her to even give a week's notice in the first place.

Rick didn't let her go home early that night. Instead, he sent one of the other girls home and had her work 'til close. She worried that he planned to harass her and try to change her mind while she cleaned up and set up the drive-thru for the next day. To her surprise, he didn't mention it even once. When she had clocked out and was ready to leave, he merely said goodnight and nodded at Paul as he walked her out to the truck where Justin was waiting.

"He didn't seem to be so worked up about your leaving," he said as they walked out to the vehicles.

"Oh, he said plenty when I gave him my notice, but he sobered up, and as you can see, he seems to be fine now. I guess it was a shock since I'd needed the job so badly. Anyway, you're not going to believe this."

"What?"

"Let me tell Justin, too." She opened the truck door and climbed up so that Justin could hear her.

Lana told them all about her day at the school and the fact that she would be available to start sooner than she had originally thought since her position was being eliminated at the school.

"Looks like we all made the right decision in the nick of time." Paul nodded his head.

"How do you feel about it, Lana?" Justin was of course the one to worry about her feelings.

"I'm good, actually. Since I had already made up my mind to take the job, I wasn't upset about it. Now if I hadn't had a job, that would have been horrible, but things have a way of working out for the best."

"I'm glad you see it that way, because I really think working for us is best for all of us." He pulled her closer and kissed her before letting her climb back out of the cab so she could ride home with Paul in her car.

After they had dropped her off at her apartment, Lana hurried through her shower so she could get into bed. Working until close during the week made it rough for her to get up the next morning to go to work. Just because she was leaving at the end of the week didn't mean she could be late in the morning.

Despite being exhausted both mentally and physically, she had trouble drifting off to sleep right away. Thoughts about how things had worked out kept circling in her head until finally she managed to slip off into a restless sleep.

Sometime later, something woke her. She didn't open her eyes. Instead, she listened for what had startled her out of sleep. At first, everything seemed fine. She couldn't hear anything out of the ordinary. There was the annoying drip of the faucet in the bathtub that the landlord refused to fix, the soft hum of the fridge in the kitchen, but she didn't notice anything else. She relaxed and chalked it up to being overtired and settled down to go back to sleep.

The sound of a single piece of glass hitting something jerked her eyes open this time. Immediately her heart began to pound and her breathing sped up. Someone was in her apartment only feet away. She was scared to move in case she made a noise. A soft crunch in the other room had her stomach threatening to empty itself of the hamburger from the night before.

She glanced over at her bedside table. It was barely three in the morning. She realized that she hadn't brought her phone into the bedroom with her for once. It was still in her purse in the living room on the couch where she'd tossed it when she got home.

She quickly assessed her options as she eased out of the bed, praying that she didn't make a noise as she did it. The only thing she could come up with was to climb through a window in order to get away. Lana didn't think she had time to put on clothes, so she crept over to the only window in her bedroom and unlocked it before attempting to open it. At first, it wouldn't budge then it slowly began to move but made a loud scraping noise she was sure the intruder would be able to hear.

Footsteps in the other room heading for the bedroom gave her the adrenaline burst she needed to finally shove the window all the way up. Just as she began to climb out, the bedroom door slammed open against the opposite wall. She screamed, but it was cut off when gloved hands grabbed at her as she tried to make it through the open window. He grabbed her by the hair and jerked her back inside, dragging her body back over the bottom of the window, scraping her back and sides on the edges. Her head hit hard on the bedframe as she tried to right herself so she could fight her captor.

Grabbing her by the throat, the man pulled her to her feet and flung her on the bed. Lana was dizzy from the lack of oxygen, so her reflexes were much slower. She attempted to roll to the other side of the bed, but the intruder grabbed one of her wrists and jerked her back toward him. He captured her other hand and taped both hands together. She started to scream but found that her throat was too sore for her to do more than moan and screech. Tape covered her mouth, but she continued to fight.

She couldn't see anything other than a pair of wild brown eyes staring down at her in the darkness. He had to be wearing a mask. She continued to try and fight him with her bound hands and kicking feet. She was so busy swinging and kicking, she never saw the blow coming that nearly knocked her out. For the few seconds that she was stunned, the stranger managed to tape her feet together as well.

Fear gurgled in her throat as she tried to regulate her breathing. She was afraid she was going to get sick and choke on her own vomit. Was this the one who'd killed that woman, or was he just a burglar?

The man disappeared from view for a few seconds, and she hoped he was going to just rob her and leave. When he returned with what looked like electrical cords she knew he wasn't just a thief. She started to roll off the bed, but he climbed up and stopped her. Then he showed her a knife, and she froze. He slipped a piece of electrical cord between her taped hands and then tied her hands above her onto the base of the bed somehow. She pulled and struggled, but it did no good.

Then he was tying her legs to each corner of the bed, having cut the tape holding them together. She struggled, kicking him with the foot that was loose until he cut her with the knife. She could feel the blood trail down her leg where he'd stabbed her. The pain didn't even register at first. Not until he was kneeling between her legs and cutting away her panties and T-shirt. Tears leaked from her eyes in a steady stream as she fought to breathe through her congested nose. When he pulled the remnants of her T-shirt from her body, Lana knew she was going to die.

He held up the knife where she could see it again before slowly dragging the flat side of it along her body between her breasts. Then he poked at her nipples with just the tip. His wild eyes told her that there was no one at home inside the mask. Tied down as she was, Lana was totally at his mercy, and hope began to slip away.

* * * *

The ringing of his cell phone on the bedside table jerked Paul awake. He grabbed the offending thing and answered it in a gravelly voice.

"Yeah."

"Paul, it's Mac Tidwell."

Thinking that someone had messed with the trench digger at the site where they were working, he groaned and ran a hand over his face.

"What's up?"

"I need you and Justin to come to the hospital as soon as you can get here."

"What the hell?" He sat up, wide awake now. "What's going on?"

There was a pause before Mac started talking again.

"Lana was attacked in her apartment. She's hysterical. I was hoping you and Justin could help calm her down so the doctor can treat her and we can talk to her."

Paul was already pulling on his jeans as Mac spoke. Fear coursed through his veins at knowing she was hurt.

"How bad is she hurt?"

"We're not sure, yet. She's covered in blood, but she won't let anyone near her."

"We're on our way." Paul slid the phone in his pants pocket and grabbed a shirt and his boots and hurried over to Justin's room.

Bursting through the door, he yelled at his brother to get his ass up and dressed. "Lana's been hurt. We need to get to the hospital."

He didn't wait for Justin's questions. Instead he hurried downstairs and finished dressing. He waited impatiently for his brother to make it downstairs. Neither man said anything until they were in the truck headed for town.

"What the fuck happened?"

Paul filled him in on what little he knew as he sped toward the hospital. Justin had one hand on the dashboard and the other one on the handhold above the door. When he parked the truck outside of the emergency room, a deputy met him at the door with his hand out.

"Give me the key so I can move your truck."

Paul handed him the key and pushed past him with Justin right behind him. He walked up to the registration window. The clerk behind the glass backed up in her chair, fear all over her face.

"Where's Lana Peters?"

"Um, she's being seen by the doctor right now. You can't go back there yet."

"The sheriff called me to come help calm her down so they could treat her. Let me the fuck back there right now."

"I–I can't, sir." She was frantically dialing someone on the phone.

"Open the fucking door, now!"

"Paul! Over here." Mac's voice reached him from around the side of the registration desk.

He and Justin hurried over to where Mac held a door open for them.

"How is she?"

"Wild. I don't think she can actually see anyone past her fear. I sure hope you can calm her down, or they're going to have to overpower her and give her something to knock her out. They don't want to do that because she's already got a head injury."

Mac pushed through the swinging door to Trauma Room Two. Paul and Justin walked in right behind him.

"Ah, hell, baby. Look at you." The sight of Lana curled up in a sheet on the floor in the corner covered in blood just about took him to his knees.

"She screams anytime someone gets close to her. Move slowly, Paul." Mac backed up and gave him plenty of room.

"Lana? It's Paul and Justin. We're here, baby. Let us see about you." He carefully approached her as he talked to her.

She stared right through him as if he wasn't even there. She was still living whatever nightmare she'd been stuck in before they got her to the hospital.

"I think we need to crawl over there instead of walking so that we're not towering over her." Justin's idea had merit.

Paul nodded and got on the floor to crawl toward her. "Lana. Listen to me, baby. It's Paul. I'm coming to get you, baby."

She whimpered, but didn't start screaming as they slowly moved closer to her. When he was within touching distance, Paul reached out and gently touched her face.

"Hey. It's just us. Everything is going to be fine, Lana. Let us help you."

Once Justin was close enough, they picked her up and gently laid her on the stretcher. When they tried to pull back so the doctor and nurses could get to her, she grabbed hold of Paul's arm and refused to let go.

"Stay there. As long as you're there, she might let us treat her. We need to see where all the blood is coming from and stop it." The doctor nodded at him.

Justin stepped back but stayed within easy reach of her should she need him. Paul stroked her hands as the nurses began to slowly pull away the bloody sheet. Paul had to grit his teeth to keep from cursing at the tiny cuts on her abdomen.

"There's the main culprit. She's been stabbed in her thigh. Move up some, sir, so we can get to it." The doctor changed places with him.

"Justin, hold her other hand. She's starting to shake all over now."

He watched as his brother eased up to the stretcher to try to take her other hand from where it had been wrapped around Paul's arm. She resisted him at first, but Justin kept whispering in her ear and she finally let him have it.

"Paul?"

He jerked his head back in her direction at the sound of her raspy voice.

"Yeah, baby. I'm right here."

"He was going to kill me."

"Shh, baby. Just relax and let the doctors fix you up."

"I was so scared. I didn't want to die."

"I know, baby. It's over. No one is ever going to hurt you again. Justin and I will take care of you."

Lana stared into his eyes then slowly closed hers and passed out. He was relieved. Looking into her eyes with all of the fear and pain in them had been gut wrenching. He looked over at Justin and knew his brother felt the same way. No one would ever hurt her again for as long as they were alive to protect her.

Chapter Nine

Lana slowly woke up to the sound of low, murmuring voices and pain. Lots of pain. Her head throbbed and her leg ached. Everything seemed fuzzy at first, then it all came back, and she sat up in bed with a scream.

"Shh, baby. You're safe. Everything is going to be fine now." Justin's voice soothed her as his hands slowly eased her back down on the stretcher.

The pounding in her head kept her from turning to look around the room, but it didn't stop her from hearing Paul and someone whose voice sounded familiar talking close by. They had stopped when she sat up, but resumed once she had settled once again. Justin didn't leave her side once she had relaxed against the stretcher. Instead, he held her hand as he listened to the other man talking. It finally dawned on her who it was as his words sank in. Sheriff Tidwell.

"One of her neighbors heard her scream and called us. We got there as soon as we could."

"Thank God you did." Paul's voice shook.

"She was unconscious when we arrived and when the paramedics loaded her up. Evidently she woke up about the time they were wheeling her into the room. They couldn't touch her until you arrived."

"Thanks for calling us, Mac. She's important to us."

"Are you and Justin claiming her, Paul?"

"Hell yes. She's ours. She won't spend another night in that hellhole."

"Good. She deserves better than that." Mac's voice sounded strained.

Justin squeezed her hand as he looked down at her. "She sure does."

She heard the swish of the door as it opened then closed. She assumed Mac had left. Lana wanted to know if they had caught the man who'd hurt her, but she was afraid to ask.

Paul's face appeared over her. His features appeared tense as he gently ran a finger along one side of her face.

"Hey, babe."

She blinked then tried to talk. "Did they catch him?" Her voice was scratchy, and her throat ached.

"Yes. They got him. He won't be hurting you ever again. I promise."

"What happened?"

"Don't worry about it. It's over and you're safe." Paul stroked her head, moving her hair away from her face.

"I need to know, Paul. What happened?"

He sighed and glanced over at Justin. She looked from one to the other of them. She wasn't going to allow them to keep anything from her. It was obvious that they didn't want to tell her something.

Finally, Paul drew in a deep breath and blew it out in a slow rush. He touched her other hand but didn't take it. She glanced down and realized that she had a tube with fluids in it running into that hand.

"When Mac and his deputies arrived, they couldn't get inside because your door was still locked. They found the window in the front broken and one of the deputies climbed through and ran straight for your bedroom. He walked in right when the man was about to stab you. He shot and killed him. You never have to worry about him again, Lana."

She closed her eyes and swallowed past the scratchiness in her throat. "Thank you. I needed to know what happened. I thought I was going to die."

"When we first saw you…" Justin's voice faded away.

She opened her eyes and looked up at him. There were tears in his eyes. From the sound of it, she had been covered in blood, hers and her attacker's. She could imagine what she looked like.

"I'm okay, though, right?"

"You're going to be fine, babe." Paul's voice brooked no argument.

"I want to go home."

"Just as soon as they discharge you, we're taking you home with us, sweetheart." Justin smiled down at her.

"How long?"

"I'll go find someone and let them know you're awake. They were waiting for you to come to before they made any decisions on whether to admit you or not." Paul turned and headed toward the door.

"Please, Paul. I don't want to stay here."

He stopped and turned to smile at her. "You'll do whatever the doctor says is best for you. No arguments." Then he walked through the swinging door.

"Don't worry. We won't leave you alone, Lana."

"Thank you. I was so scared, Justin."

"I know. But you don't have to be anymore. We'll take care of you."

She closed her eyes once again to wait for Paul to return. She didn't want to stay in the hospital. It brought back too many sad memories of when her mom was dying. As small as the hospital was, she might even end up in the same room. That thought had her heart racing once again, and she started to shiver.

"Are you cold?" Justin asked.

"No. I guess I'm just nervous. I want to go home. I don't want to be here anymore."

"I know. Paul will be back in a few minutes."

The swinging door to the room opened, and several people walked in with Paul leading the small group. He had a grim, determined expression on his face.

"Hi, Lana. It's good to see you awake and resting. I'm Dr. Deering. How are you feeling?" The stranger was nice looking with a genuine smile that reached his hazel eyes. His light brown hair was short but mussed as if he'd just run his hand through it.

"Fine. I want to go home."

"Let's check you out and we'll see." He looked up and a nurse began checking her blood pressure while he checked her eyes and had her follow directions and answer silly questions.

After a few minutes of examining her and conferring with the nurse, he smiled down at her.

"I think it would be safe for you to go home as long as someone will be there to wake you up every few hours and check on you. You have a good-sized knot on your head, so I'm a little worried about a mild concussion."

"She'll be going home with us. We'll take care of her." Paul's deep voice interrupted them.

"Good, good." He smiled down at her. "It looks like you'll be in good hands. I'm going to write a prescription for some antibiotics and a pain pill you can take starting around two this afternoon. We'll give you some Tylenol for your headache. I'm sure you have one."

At her nod, he looked over at the nurse. She quickly disappeared through the door only to return in a few seconds with two pills and a cup of water. Justin helped her lift up enough to take the pills and drink the water. They scratched her throat on the way down. She guessed her throat was sore from screaming.

"Okay, I've written your prescriptions and your discharge orders. Let the nurse take out your IV and get your paperwork finished and you can leave. You need to follow up with your own physician in five to six days to see about removing the stitches."

"Stitches?" Her eyes settled on Paul. "I didn't know I had stitches."

The doctor smiled and started telling her about her injuries. "You've got a bruised throat from being strangled and probably from screaming as well. You've got four stitches in your head up here." He pointed to her forehead.

She reached up with one hand to feel, but the doctor stopped her hand in midair.

"Don't touch the area. I have a small bandage on it, but it's going to be tender. You shouldn't be able to see it under your bangs, and it shouldn't leave much of a scar." He patted her hand. "You've got a stab wound to your right upper thigh that we left open to heal naturally. It's covered in a bandage as well. You also have some small cuts on your abdomen, but none of them needed stitches. There is some bruising along your ribs on the right side and your right shoulder and down your back, but nothing was broken."

Lana shivered at the list of her injuries. She knew she was sore all over, but she hadn't really thought about what hurt or why other than her throat and her head.

"I want you to get lots of rest over the next few days then follow your primary physician's orders after that. Understand?" He looked down at her and smiled before nodding at Paul and Justin as he turned to go.

They nurse began taking the IV out of her hand, covering it with a small bandage once she was finished.

"I'll go get your paperwork finished and find you a set of scrubs to wear home. Then we'll get you out of here." She winked at her before leaving her alone with the men.

"Not much longer, sweetheart. We'll have you home before you know it." Justin's concerned expression was almost more than she could take.

She squeezed her eyes shut to stop the tears. Too much had happened, and she felt like an emotional wreck. She didn't want to cry anymore. She remembered crying when…She didn't want to remember that, either.

"Shh, babe. Everything is going to be fine. Once we get you home we'll help you clean up and then settle you down in the bed so you can rest. You'll feel better once you've had some sleep."

Lana wasn't so sure about that. She was a little afraid to fall asleep, certain that when she did it would come back to her in her dreams.

After about fifteen minutes, the nurse returned with her paperwork and a set of scrubs for her to put on. The nurse reviewed the paperwork with them and had Lana sign the discharge form before leaving so she could get dressed. Lana had refused her help, believing she could dress herself. When she started to get down off the stretcher, Justin and Paul were immediately by her side helping her down.

"You can wait outside while I dress, guys."

"We're not leaving you to do this alone. You're weak, babe. You could fall."

She frowned up at them and started to cross her arms, but pain in her ribs and her right shoulder stopped her.

"See, you're sore all over. Let us help you."

Lana sighed and nodded. She realized that she probably did need the help. She should have asked the nurse to help her. Instead, she found herself letting them help her remove the gown, holding it to her breasts as they settled the scrub top over her head. Then they pulled the pants up her legs but let her tie the drawstrings herself. By the time they were finished, she was worn out and shaking. As much as she didn't like to admit it, she had needed help.

Justin left her with Paul to pull the truck up outside the emergency room then a nurse pushed her out in a wheelchair, Paul following behind with her paperwork and prescriptions. He picked her up and sat her on the seat in the truck then climbed in next to her. Once they were all buckled up, Justin pulled out of the hospital. Lana immediately felt better to be away from the place.

They pulled up outside the local pharmacy, and Paul took the prescriptions inside to have them filled. While they waited, Justin stroked her hair and told her about the yard they were working on outside of town. Before she realized it, Paul was back with her medications and they started out once again.

It suddenly dawned on her that they were driving in the opposite direction of her apartment. She quickly realized they were headed toward their house. She looked over at Justin then back at Paul.

"Why are we going to your place? I want to go home."

"First of all, you can't right now, because it's a crime scene and the sheriff's department is there. Second of all, you don't have a window in the living room, so you can't stay there for obvious reasons." Paul squeezed her hand before bringing it to his lips and kissing it.

"Oh." She didn't know what more she could say to that. "What about my clothes?"

"They wouldn't let you take anything from there anyway. You can wear something of ours until they let us get your things."

She rolled her eyes. Like anything of theirs would fit her. They were over six feet each, and she had curves. Oh well, the scrubs would do for now. She should be able to get to her things soon enough.

Once they arrived at the house, Paul helped her out of the truck and carried her inside despite her protests. Justin led the way upstairs and turned down the bed in the master bedroom. She tried to protest, but they pointed out that they didn't have another room for her to sleep in. Justin gently laid her down and pulled the covers up to her waist before kissing her lightly on the lips.

The bed felt wonderful to her aching body. She knew Justin was working hard not to tease her about her sigh of appreciation by the grin on his face. She stuck her tongue out at him despite it being juvenile.

"How about something to eat?" Paul held up one of the bottles of pills she was supposed to take. "It says here you should take them with food. What sounds good to you?"

"My throat hurts, so I'm not sure what I could eat. I'm not really hungry."

"How about scrambled eggs?" Justin suggested.

"That sounds good. I could probably manage eggs. Thanks."

He hurried out the door, leaving her alone with Paul. He eased down on the side of the bed and smiled at her. She realized that she hadn't seen him smile all that often. It gave him a much younger look to his face, smoothing out all the harsh lines that were normally there.

"Oh, I need to call the school to let them know I'm not going to be there." Panic grabbed her as she looked at the time on the clock by the bed.

"Don't worry about it. Justin called them earlier as soon as someone answered. He told them you wouldn't be back at all this week."

"What? I can't leave them like that. It's my last week. I need to be there to tie stuff up."

Paul frowned at her. "You're hurt, Lana. You can't work like that. Maybe if you're feeling better on Friday, you can go for a few hours and square things away. We'll see how you're doing then."

"Paul, you can't tell me what I can and can't do."

"Watch me. You're our responsibility now. We will make whatever decisions we think necessary to keep you safe and healthy."

"I am *not* your responsibility. I can take care of myself." She couldn't believe he was being so arrogant.

"Arguing already?" Justin walked in carrying a plate full of fluffy scrambled eggs and a glass of milk.

He waited while Paul helped her sit back up, propping a pillow behind her for support before he handed her the plate. Then he set the glass of milk on the bedside table. They both stood back and watched her as she prepared to dig in. She looked up and cocked a brow at them.

"What? Did I forget something?" Justin asked.

"Are you going to stand there and stare at me? I can't eat with you doing that. Don't you have something you need to be doing? Like go to work?"

Justin chuckled. "We took the day off to see about you. We're not leaving you alone when you've just gotten out of the hospital from being attacked."

She resisted the urge to growl. They were taking things entirely too seriously now. She was fine. They didn't need to hang over her no matter how sweet it sounded.

"Why don't you go get something to eat? You're bound to be hungry as well."

Paul shrugged. "We can wait until you're finished. You might need something."

Since she had never had anyone to watch over her before, she didn't know how to react. It was obvious that they cared about her. It thrilled her on one level and worried her on another one. Hopefully, they would lighten up as she proved to them that she was okay. Until then, it looked like she was stuck with an audience to watch her eat and rest. Maybe it wouldn't be so bad.

Chapter Ten

She was going crazy. They hadn't left her alone all day long. Even when she had fallen asleep, it was to find at least one of them there waiting on her to wake up again. It was as bad as actually being in the hospital, she decided. Wasn't it driving them crazy just sitting there doing nothing?

She needed to go to the bathroom and dreaded what sort of drama that would cause. She didn't know whether to just get up and walk in that direction or ask permission. It irked her to no end that she felt like a prisoner. Well, she wasn't going to act like one. She threw the covers off and started to swing her legs over the edge of the bed. Before she had even gotten one toe off, Paul was by her side.

"What are you doing?"

"I need to go to the bathroom, and I don't need help to do that."

"You can't walk on that leg. I'll carry you."

"I can walk, Paul. I'm not an invalid." She stood up despite his attempts to stop her and smiled at him.

As soon as she took a step using her injured leg, the pain nearly caused her to pass out. She would have hit the floor had Paul not been ready to catch her. To his credit, he didn't look smug or say *I told you so*. Instead, he effortlessly carried her into the bathroom and stood her by the toilet.

"Thanks. I can get it from here." She refused to look at him before he turned and left her, closing the door softly behind him.

"Just call me when you're finished, Lana. I'll wait right here for you." She cringed, knowing if she could hear him through the door he could hear her as well.

After finishing, she stood up and hopped over to the sink to wash her hands then she called out for Paul. He didn't say anything about how she'd gotten to the sink, only lifted an eyebrow and shook his head before picking her up once again. She could tell he was frustrated with her refusal to admit that she needed assistance. She couldn't help it. She'd always taken care of herself and later, her mom. It was a part of her, and asking for assistance with something as simple as getting to the bathroom just didn't sit well with her.

He didn't return her to the bed, much to her surprise. Instead, he carried her into the living room and settled her on the couch, covering her with a throw off the back of the couch.

"I'm going to start dinner. I can't trust you to stay in bed, so I figured that letting you stay on the couch is a good compromise. I can watch you, and you aren't all alone in the bedroom to think up ways to get into trouble."

She gasped. "I don't do that."

His mouth turned up in a small smile before he covered it up. "It seems like it. Now rest while I cook. We can talk if you want to."

She watched him walk toward the kitchen and instantly missed his presence near her. She huffed out a breath and situated herself on the couch to her satisfaction. She realized that she hadn't seen Justin in a few hours and wondered where he was.

"Paul? Where is Justin?"

"Do you miss him, babe?"

"Just wondering where he is."

"He'll be back in a little while."

She frowned. That didn't tell her where he was. Not that it was any of her business what he did with his time, but they had said they had taken off to take care of her today. It hit her that she was being a baby now.

"When were you supposed to work at The Burger Hop again?" Paul's voice pulled her from her musings.

"I work Thursday and Friday nights 'til close."

"We better call Rick and let him know you're not going to be able to work it. You can't stand on your leg like that."

It was right on the tip of her tongue to tell Paul he couldn't tell her what to do, but in this instance, he was right. She wouldn't be able to handle several hours, much less four or five on her injured leg.

"You're right. I'll call him now so he'll have time to find someone to cover my shifts." She started to get up then thought better of it. "Can I borrow your phone, Paul?"

"Good girl." His full smile transformed his normally stoic expression into something amazing. "I'll bring it to you."

She couldn't help but stare at him when he held out his cell phone for her to use. He was even more handsome than she had originally thought.

"Um, Lana?"

She closed her mouth and took the phone. "Thanks."

She watched as he nodded and headed back to the kitchen. She quickly dialed the number to The Burger Hop and waited for someone to answer. One of the employees picked up and put her on hold while they got Rick on the line.

"This is Rick."

"Rick, it's Lana. I've hurt my leg and won't be able to work Thursday or Friday after all. I'm really sorry…"

"What happened? How did you get hurt?"

"Someone broke into my apartment and attacked me. I'm okay, but I won't be able to cover my shift after all."

"Are you sure you're okay? Do you need anything?" Rick actually sounded worried. It threw her for a loop.

"I'm fine, Rick. I'm staying with Paul and Justin. They wouldn't let me back in my apartment yet." There was silence on the other end of the phone for a few seconds. "Rick? Are you still there?"

"You know that if word gets out that you are staying with them everyone will believe you're sleeping with them."

"Rick. It really doesn't matter what anyone else thinks. It's none of their business what I do with my life."

"Lana, just because there are other people living that way around Riverbend doesn't mean it's right. Let me come get you. You can stay with me."

She could feel her blood pressure rise. He seemed to think it was okay for her to stay with him but not with Paul and Justin. They had been nothing but good to her. There was no way she would stay with Rick instead of with them after all that they had done for her.

"Rick. Thank you for worrying about me, but I'm fine. I'm going to stay here until they let me back in my apartment. I need to go now. Bye." She didn't wait for his answer. Instead she hit *off* and struggled to get her anger under control.

Paul walked back in and sat on the couch next to her. She handed him the phone and forced a smile.

"Thanks. That's taken care of."

"He upset you. What did he say?"

"Nothing to worry about. He just didn't like that I was staying here."

She watched as Paul's face hardened. She could see the pulse beating in the vein at his temple. He didn't like that she hadn't told him what Rick had said, but it was none of his business.

"Justin should be back soon, and dinner is about ready. I made spaghetti. I thought it would be fairly easy on your throat."

She couldn't help but smile at him for thinking about how she would be able to swallow her food. He and Justin were thoughtful like that, even if they could be exasperating as well. He held her hand and carried it to his lips. The gentle gesture nearly brought tears to her eyes. Staying angry with them was next to impossible when they did little things like that. She quickly blinked her eyes to clear them.

Paul leaned in closer and brushed his lips across hers. He never closed his eyes. She felt trapped by the heated gaze as he left no doubt that he wanted her. When she swayed closer to him, a noise in the kitchen jarred her away from him.

"Hey. Something smells good." Justin walked into the living room carrying her suitcase and a large box.

"It's about time you got back. Dinner is ready." Paul stood up and took the box from Justin's arms. "I'll help you take this up to the bedroom. Lana, we'll be back down in a second."

"Wait! What are you doing with my suitcase? Did they let you in my apartment? Can I go home now?" No way was she letting them get by with this.

"We'll talk about it while we're eating. I'll tell you all about it." Justin kept walking toward the stairs with Paul following him.

"You're damn right we will." She realized she was talking to their butts as they climbed the steps.

Exasperated, she crossed her arms and waited for them to return. Several long minutes later, they walked back down. Paul had a small, smug smile while Justin's was broad. They were definitely up to something. She would put a stop to it, though. She was not going to stay with them any longer than necessary, and it looked like it was no longer necessary from what she could see.

Before she could start in on them again, Justin picked her up off the couch, carrying her to the kitchen. He settled her at the table that Paul had already set. Paul began serving the food and took a seat to one side of her. His brother took the one on the other side. They dug in as soon as they had their plates fixed. Lana held back. She had every intention of finding out what was going on with her apartment.

"So? What's going on?" She directed her question to Justin.

Justin glanced over at Paul before answering. "Well, they let me go in and get a few things for you, but they haven't released the crime scene yet. I had to go in with one of the deputies and couldn't touch anything except what he cleared for me to."

"When will my apartment be free again? I need to see about getting the window fixed."

"Eat before it gets cold, Lana," Paul said.

She frowned at him but took a bite of her spaghetti. It was delicious. She couldn't help but be surprised that he was such a good cook. Before she could compliment him on it, Justin spoke again.

"I'm not real sure when they will let it go. They called in a crime unit from Dallas since they think it's related to that murder the other weekend."

"I wish I had been able to go with you." She was pretty sure Justin wouldn't have gotten what she needed if she was going to be there a few days.

"If I missed something you need, we can call Mac and run back over there for it, sweetheart. Don't worry about it. You're welcome here for as long as it takes."

That was what she was afraid of. Staying with them wasn't going to be easy. She was much too attracted to them, and they were very aggressive in their attempts at seducing her. She knew she wouldn't be able to resist them for long, and her injuries wouldn't protect her from their attentions. She needed the job. Succumbing to their wiles was the fastest way to losing it.

The brothers talked back and forth about the job they were working on while they ate. Lana only halfway paid attention to their conversation. She had too much on her mind right then. She needed to pay bills for one thing, and since she was already there, she figured she might as well start looking around in the office to see what she would need to start on first. She had no doubt it would take several days just to organize the mess. The sooner she got started, the sooner she could get everything in order.

"Lana? Did you hear me?" Paul's amused voice got her attention.

"No, sorry. I was just thinking that while I was here I should go ahead and get started in the office."

"You're injured, Lana. You need to rest and heal." Justin frowned at her.

"I was asking if you wanted some more to eat." Paul pointed to her empty plate.

"Thanks. It was really good, but I'm full." She leaned back from the table and patted her stomach.

"You don't eat enough, sweetheart." Justin seemed to be the one fussing at her today.

She refrained from rolling her eyes since it seemed childish under the circumstances. It wasn't like she couldn't stand to lose a few pounds even if she wasn't full. She had a feeling she would be read the riot act if she made that comment out loud though, so she chose to ignore it.

"I can sit in the chair in the office and go through the paperwork to get it organized. I'm going to get tired of sitting here doing nothing, and no way am I staying in bed all day tomorrow."

"I brought your Kindle for you to read. That will give you something to do while you're healing." Justin grinned at her, obviously pleased with himself.

She was getting nowhere with them right now. She would bring it up again in the morning. There was no use in arguing with them now, especially since she was yawning. Her nap earlier had only perked her up for a few hours. She obviously needed more sleep to make up for what she lost the night before.

"Looks like you're about ready to go to bed, babe. I'll help you get settled." Paul stood up and picked her up from the chair.

"I feel funny having you carry me everywhere."

"Nonsense. You can't walk on that leg yet. Give it time to heal up before you put too much pressure on it. Besides, we like carrying you around. Isn't that right, Justin?" Paul looked over his shoulder at his brother.

"Sure is. I like having you in my arms."

She remained quiet as he carried her upstairs to the bedroom. When he settled her on the bed, she sighed. As much as she hated staying in bed, right now it felt good to be back. She hadn't realized how tired she actually was. At least her head wasn't hurting much now. The dull ache was bearable.

Paul pulled up the covers and bent down to kiss her. She couldn't stop herself from digging her hands into his hair to prolong the kiss. She blamed it on how tired she was that she hadn't been able to resist the need. When Justin took Paul's place and covered her mouth with his, she moaned and squeezed his shoulders. By the time he'd pulled back, her pussy was wet and her nipples were poking against her top and the covers.

"Good night, Lana. We'll check on you before we head to bed in a little while. Just call out if you need us. We'll hear you." Paul clicked off the light and closed the door.

There was a small light on in the bathroom so she wasn't totally in the dark. It was comforting for some reason. She'd never been afraid of the dark before, but maybe she needed that light for now. After all, she was in a strange house and had been attacked less than twenty-four hours ago. A night-light wasn't anything major to obsess over.

Lana snuggled into the covers, and clearing her mind, she promptly fell asleep.

Chapter Eleven

The scream jerked Justin awake from a deep sleep. Having Lana in their home and in their care had lulled him into some of the best sleep he'd had in a long time. The shrill scream had him out of the bed and running to the master bedroom even before his eyes were fully open. He nearly crashed into Paul as he entered the room.

They reached the bed and a thrashing Lana in mere seconds, but to Justin it had seemed like long minutes. She was fighting the covers and crying uncontrollably. It broke his heart to hear her screams and pleading.

"Shh, Lana. It's okay, sweetheart. We've got you. You're safe."

Paul had her arms, trying to keep her from hitting herself or them as she fought her imaginary assailant. He wrapped his arms around her middle and tried to calm her.

"You're safe, Lana. Wake up. Everything is okay."

Paul swore when she finally stopped fighting, but the crying didn't cease.

"Fuck, baby. Wake up. You're killing me."

Finally, she opened her eyes. After a couple of seconds, she seemed to focus on them and wrapped her arms around Justin. After a few more seconds she pulled back and looked over at Paul.

"I'm sorry. I didn't mean to wake you both up."

"Shh, babe. It's okay. It was a bad dream. You couldn't help it." Paul ran a hand down her hair.

She looked from one to the other and shivered. "Please don't leave me alone."

Justin nodded at Paul and they both climbed into bed with her. He snuggled up against her back as she wrapped her arm over Paul's bare chest. When his cock nestled against her lower back, she stiffened as if she had just realized they were nude. Since she was dressed, he hoped she wouldn't see it as an issue.

"Easy, sweetheart. It's all fine. We're not going to hurt you. Just relax and go back to sleep." He kissed her shoulder and waited for her to slowly relax against him.

"You're hard."

"I'm always hard around you, Lana. We both are. Don't worry about it. Go to sleep."

"I'm sorry." Her whispered apology sounded so sweet and innocent.

"Nothing to be sorry about, babe." Paul's deep assurance seemed to settle her some.

Justin heard her soft sigh as she moved between them. His arm over her waist felt good there. He could tell that she was wrapped around Paul. He made sure he kept his legs from bumping against her thigh. He didn't want to jostle her injured one.

After a few minutes, he felt her relax entirely back into sleep. She had a soft snore that was cute. He lay there for a few minutes thinking about how much he was already in love with her and how they would have to be very careful to keep from scaring her off after what had happened to her. Somehow they had to convince her to move in with them and keep her out of that fire trap of an apartment. He didn't want her spending another night in that building.

He'd asked Mac to keep her apartment off-limits for her as long as possible. The sheriff had agreed and said that it wouldn't be that difficult since there was an ongoing investigation due to the recent murder and the fact that the suspect had been killed there. They would have another couple of days for sure.

The bastard had been connected to murders all over the Midwest involving young, single women who lived alone and were vulnerable.

From what they had been able to piece together with the help of the FBI, the man was a serial killer who would never hurt another woman again. Although he was pleased that the son of a bitch was dead, he wished he'd been the one to have squeezed the trigger. He had hurt his woman.

Justin nuzzled his face against Lana's hair and breathed in her unique scent of mint and cinnamon. He knew part of it came from her shampoo, but not all of it. The rest was just her. He couldn't get enough of being near her.

Finally, he relaxed enough to drift off, but he remained alert enough that if she moved, he would wake up. He had no doubt that Paul, with his military background, would be sleeping much the same way. He knew she was safe between them, but despite that, he wouldn't let down his guard around her.

* * * *

Lana woke up feeling much better than she had expected to after the nightmare. She stretched and realized that the men were already gone. She was secretly happy and sad. Part of her wanted to wake up between them while the other part of her was glad not to have to deal with the uneasiness it would have caused for her. It had been obvious that they were naked when they had climbed into bed with her.

She sighed. They had acted like perfect gentlemen, though. For some reason, that disappointed her to some extent. She didn't think she had been ready for them to try anything, but the fact that they hadn't made her wonder if they really did want her.

Justin's cock was hard against you, Lana. Does that sound like a man who isn't interested in you?

She pushed back the covers and started to get up only to remember how sore she was. Looking around, she realized that neither one of the men was there to watch her for a change. She grinned. That meant she could go to the bathroom by herself.

Lana carefully stood up by the side of the bed and tested her injured leg. It gave a definite twinge, but she thought if she was careful, she would be able to hobble to the bathroom on her own.

Thirty minutes later, she was showered and ready to get dressed. She hobbled out of the bathroom to find Justin waiting on her with a scowl on his face.

"What are you doing standing on your bad leg? You should have waited for me." He scooped her up and carried her back to the bed.

"I made it just fine. I can't depend on you for everything, Justin. Aren't you supposed to go back to work today?" She made a face at him when he crossed his arms after sat her on the bed.

"Paul's working today. I'm staying with you. We can't trust you to take it easy without one of us watching over you."

"I don't need a babysitter." She frowned at him.

"Sit right there and I'll find you something to put on." He ignored her babysitting comment and turned to the dresser where they'd stashed her clothes the night before.

He handed her a pair of shorts and a loose T-shirt. She took them but continued to stare at him.

"What?"

"Where's my underwear?"

He looked sheepish. "Um, I didn't remember to get any when I got your clothes. Sorry."

"You didn't get me underwear? How am I supposed to dress without it? I can't go anywhere without a bra." She couldn't help the growl that escaped.

"Don't worry. You're not going to be going anywhere anytime soon. I'm sure we can get some by then. You don't have to wear any here with us, sweetheart."

Now Lana wasn't so sure it had been a mistake. She narrowed her eyes at him. He had the grace to blush at her scrutiny. Yeah, it looked like he was guilty of something all right. She had a sneaky suspicion that Justin was a handful in and out of bed. That thought brought heat rising in her cheeks.

"Hurry up and dress, sweetheart. I have breakfast ready for you. Do you want some help?"

"I can dress by myself. Out." She watched him walk back through the door and close the door behind him.

"I'll be right out here in case you need me. You can't go down the stairs without me."

Lana didn't bother answering him. She hurried to get her shorts and T-shirt on before he decided to come back in. She didn't think she could help herself if he were to walk in on her without her clothes on.

She noted that she didn't have shoes or socks. She hobbled over to the door and opened it. Justin smiled and scooped her up in his arms.

"Hold on. We'll be downstairs before you know it." He winked at her and carried her slowly down the stairs.

She could feel the strength in his muscles as they flexed beneath her. Her size bothered her, and she was half-afraid he would lose his grip or stumble while carrying her downstairs. When he deposited her safely at the table in the kitchen, she breathed a sigh of relief. She realized he wasn't even winded when he bent down and kissed her lightly on the lips.

After breakfast, Justin chatted with her while he cleaned up the kitchen then suggested she relax on the couch for a while with her Kindle. Lana wanted to see about the paperwork in the office, but decided to wait and pursue that after lunch. With any luck, she could coax some information from Justin about him and Paul. She knew next to nothing about them.

Justin settled her on the couch with her feet in his lap. He gently massaged them while they chatted. She liked how relaxed and easy he was to be around. Paul was a bit intimidating and reserved. She wasn't afraid of either of them, but sometimes she wasn't sure of how Paul felt about things.

"How long have you and Paul lived here?"

"We were born here. Our mom and dads live here but are out exploring in their camper this summer. Last time we heard from them they were in Colorado."

"Dads?" she managed to squeak out.

"Yeah. We have two dads. It was great growing up to always have one of them around to help figure something out or for advice." He grinned at her from across the couch. "Wasn't so hot though when we were in trouble."

"I can't imagine having two. Mine left when I was four. My mom raised me." She realized that they came about their expectation to live the ménage lifestyle naturally with having grown up in one.

"That's tough. I can't imagine life without either one of them." He had stopped massaging her feet and had one hand on her lower leg with the other along the back of the couch.

Lana just nodded, at a loss as to what to ask next. Justin didn't seem to have that problem, though.

"How come you've never gotten married? You're a beautiful woman, Lana."

"I really haven't dated much. I was busy with school and then with taking care of Mom. There just wasn't a lot of time for a social life."

She picked up her Kindle with the intention of reading and putting an end to the questions. She hadn't figured that he would get personal. She knew it wasn't fair when she wanted to know so much more about them.

Justin seemed fine with sitting there while she read for a long time. After about an hour, he patted her leg and stood up, repositioning her feet on the couch.

"I'm going to grab something to drink. Do you want a Diet Coke?"

"That would be wonderful, thanks." She smiled up at him and he returned the smile before walking to the kitchen.

A few seconds later, he returned with a glass of iced tea for himself and a Diet Coke for her.

"Why do you have these here? Neither one of you seems to drink them."

"For you, sweetheart. We want to have what you like here for when you're around."

"Oh." She wasn't sure what to say to that.

Justin set his glass on a coaster on the end table and crouched down in front of the couch. He took her drink and located another coaster for it next to his. He took her hands in his and stared into her eyes.

"Lana. You know we are attracted to you. We want to know everything about you we can. Don't close up on us, hon." He leaned in and took her lips in a soft kiss.

Lana couldn't help but respond to him. Her mouth opened and his tongue dove inside to tease and tangle with hers. She slipped her hands into his hair and gave herself over to him with a whimper as he took her higher and higher with just the kiss. Then he was pulling away just enough to run his mouth all along her jaw to nip and suck on her earlobe. It sent shivers down her spine and goose bumps along her arms. She could feel her pussy weeping her juice as Justin continued his roving down her neck.

He licked at her neck then sucked on it, no doubt leaving a mark there before moving over to her shoulder. He nuzzled aside the neck of the V-neck T-shirt she was wearing and bit lightly against her shoulder. Pulling back, he looked deep into her eyes.

"Let me give you pleasure, Lana. I want to show you how much you mean to me. To us. I'll be careful with you. Please, sweetheart. Let me taste your sweet honey."

"Oh, God, Justin. What are you doing to me? I can't breathe."

"Shh. Just relax and let me make you feel good. I'll take real good care of you, Lana." He moved down her body and slipped his hands beneath her shirt to lightly rasp over her nipples. They were already hard from his kisses, but with the extra stimulation, they began to ache in need for a heavier touch. Justin lifted the cotton material and folded it at her neck. He just stared at her breasts for several seconds before moaning and lowering his mouth to lick at one torrid peak. The sensation of his tongue rasping over the tip sent jolts of electricity through her body.

"God, they're perfect, Lana." He palmed them with his large hands then sucked a nipple deep into his mouth.

Lana bowed her back as he sucked more and more of her breast into his mouth. He seemed on a mission to take all he could into the hot, wet cavern before finally backing off to nip at the nipple once more. Then he moved to the other breast and repeated the process while pulling and rolling the abandoned one between his fingers.

It was too much. Lana felt things begin to simmer deep inside of her. If he kept doing what he was doing, she was going to come from him playing with her breasts alone. That shouldn't happen, should it? He would think she was immature if that happened. She fought it with all her strength, but when he lightly bit and pulled on her nipple, electricity arced across her body, sending her pussy into spasms.

"Ahhh!" She screamed out her climax even as tears spilled down her face with embarrassment.

Justin growled around her nipple before releasing it and sitting back. When he saw her tears he cupped her face with both hands.

"Shh, what's wrong, sweetheart? Did I hurt you? God, baby. What's wrong?"

"I–I couldn't stop it. I'm sorry." She turned her face from him, sure that she would see disgust in his face.

"Oh, honey. Don't apologize for that. It was the most amazing thing I've ever experienced. You're so responsive, hon. I love it." He kissed her cheeks and thumbed away the tears there.

"You're not disappointed with me?"

"Hell, no. That was wonderful, but I'm not through with you yet." He kissed her again then grinned and began kissing his way down her chest and abdomen, making sure to skirt the tiny cuts there, to the waistband of her shorts.

Lana moaned as his mouth caressed her pelvis. When he began pulling down her shorts, she panicked. Her shorts were wet from her arousal. What would he think of her? He growled when she grabbed his hands to stop him.

"Move your hands, sweetheart. I've got to taste your sweet honey. I can smell you and it's driving me crazy."

She lifted them and sighed when he pulled her shorts from her body. Justin moved one leg out and over his shoulder so that he could access her wet center. His warm breath across he pussy lips made her jerk with anticipation of more. Surely he would drive her insane if he touched her there. She was already panting with expectation as his mouth hovered mere inches from her most intimate of places.

The second his mouth kissed her there, Lana felt as if every nerve ending in her body quivered at one time. She cried out in frustration when he didn't immediately consume her.

Chapter Twelve

"Easy, Lana. I'll take care of you. I'll make you feel so good. Shh, hon."

He breathed in her scent. It went straight to his head as he held her still with one hand above her mons since her abdomen had cuts across it. Leaning in once again, he licked her sweet slit up to her clit then circled the little bud that had protruded from its hood. Her soft whimpers and quick jerks let him know that she was already on her way to the bliss he wanted to give her.

He spread her pussy lips and lapped at the cream-slicked folds before stabbing delicately into her cunt. The more he plunged into her tight sheath, the more he wanted to bury his cock there. She was hot and wet and tight. He entered her with one finger, and her inner muscles grabbed at him as if wanting to keep him there. He added a second finger and marveled at how snug she was. His cock twitched at the promise of all of her wet, feminine heat surrounding it soon.

He slowly pumped his fingers in and out of her several times before curving them and locating her hot spot. She jerked and moaned with each stroke over the spongy tissue. He leaned in and licked her once again in an effort to gain more of her juices.

"Justin! I can't take it. It's too much."

"Yes you can, sweetheart. Let go and feel how good it can be."

She groaned when he thrust his fingers back inside of her pussy and stroked her G-spot over and over until she was undulating in an effort to capture more of the intoxicating sensation he was giving her. He knew she was close by the way her breathing had increased. He sucked in her clit and nibbled at it until she screamed his name as her leg hooked around his neck and held him against her pulsing folds.

Justin lapped up her cream until she slowly relaxed then collapsed back against the couch. He extracted himself from her leggy embrace and returned to the top of the couch to take her mouth in another kiss, sharing her essence with her.

"That was beautiful, Lana. You're so passionate. I love hearing my name on your lips."

"I've never…Oh, God. It was wonderful." Her eyes flew open and panic filled them. "What about Paul? Won't he be angry?"

"No, baby. He'll just be jealous that he wasn't here to at least watch. We want to share you between us. Sometimes together and sometimes separately. You have nothing to worry about."

She smiled shyly at him before reaching up with one hand and caressing his cheek. It was a soft touch that only made him harder because it was freely given. He took her hand and kissed the palm before standing up and retrieving her discarded shorts.

"I'll run and get you another pair. These would be uncomfortable as wet as they are." He chuckled at her quick blush.

When he returned it was to find her standing on one leg by the couch waiting on him. He quickly pulled her shorts up and settled her back on the couch with her Kindle. After kissing her forehead, he left her there to start lunch. He wasn't a good cook like Paul, but he was able to manage a few things. He decided on sandwiches for lunch since they would be essentially foolproof. Plus, he didn't want to waste any time he had with her in the kitchen.

Justin had to adjust his cock in order to stand at the bar making the sandwiches so it wouldn't poke out against the unforgiving wood. He knew it was too soon after Lana's attack, but he couldn't wait for when they could take her between them. She was so responsive and beautiful in her passion. He couldn't wait to tell Paul about it. As soon as he got her settled in the office, he planned to call his brother and share the experience.

He had already decided to let her work in the office some as long as she swore she wouldn't stand on her leg any. It would help her keep her mind off of what had happened and make her feel useful at the same time. He could see the struggle in her expressive face on how to handle working for them while they courted her at the same time. She fancied herself planning to keep them at arm's length. That was part of the reason he had pleasured her earlier, to get that notion out of her head. The other reason was pure selfishness. He had to taste her.

When he finished the sandwiches and had the chips out for her to choose from, Justin returned to the living room and carried her to the table. They talked about mundane things like the extreme heat and lack of rain. He told her a little more about growing up in Riverbend. She seemed fascinated by his stories about him and Paul.

After cleaning up, Justin carried her to the office off of the living room and helped her start on the paperwork. She caught on quickly and soon he was able to slip out while she worked. He called Paul from the kitchen. His brother answered on the second ring.

"Hey, is she doing okay?"

"She's fine, bro. Everything working out okay at the site?"

"No problem so far. Looks like we're going to be right on time. Just wish this heat would let up some."

Justin could imagine how hard it was working out in it. He was usually there right along with Paul.

"Keep hydrated. Don't need you passing out with heat stroke. Did you get both coolers full of water?"

"I got them. We're all doing fine. What's going on there?"

"Lana's working in the office. I figure it will help keep her mind off of the attack."

"Good idea. I hate for her to work when she should be resting, though."

"I'll make sure she takes a nap before you get home. What time do you plan to make it?"

Paul hesitated for a brief second. "It's probably going to be a little late. I want to finish up with the trench digger today so we can return it to the rental place tonight. No use wasting a day's rent on it for nothing."

"I agree. I'll plan for a late dinner. What about seven?"

"Sounds good. I should be there by six and be able to get showered in time." Paul's voice grew quieter. "How is she responding to you?"

"Much better than before. I got her to relax enough that I could taste her sweet pussy and make her come."

"Fuck! I wish I had been there for that. How does she taste?" Paul's voice had gone deeper.

"Like liquid gold. She's so fucking responsive, Paul. You're going to love the sounds she makes when she's all riled up. I nearly came in my jeans just hearing her scream out my name."

"I can't wait to get home now. I'm going to eat her up for dessert."

Justin grinned. "I'll make sure she's ready for you. I better go and check on her. I'll see you tonight."

He pushed *off* before shoving the phone back on his belt in the holder. Then he headed back to the office to check on his little Lana.

* * * *

Lana didn't bother to look up when Justin walked back in after having disappeared earlier. She was too busy sorting papers into piles. She was almost finished with that part and planned to conquer filing them the next day. First she had to determine their filing system–or lack of one. The opened drawers and half-shoved-in papers didn't give her much hope on that front.

She rolled the chair closer to one of the file cabinets and stood up on her good leg. The top file drawer was pretty much over her head. She needed a stool. She sighed. The top drawer would have to wait until later. She closed it the best she could and pulled out the next drawer.

"We'll get you a stool for the top drawer when you're able to stand on two feet again. No way you're climbing with one leg."

Lana bit her lower lip to keep from smiling and ignored him. She needed to concentrate on learning the office and not think about what had taken place on the couch earlier. Her face grew hot at the brief thought. What was she going to do if just being in the same room with one of them had her thinking dirty thoughts?

She pulled out some of the files and sat back on the chair to scoot over to the desk where she could go through them and see what they were. There was nothing on the front of the file drawer to give her a clue as to what was supposed to be in it. It took a minute, but finally she managed to get back into reading. Still, she knew the second he'd gotten up and walked out of the room. A part of her had wanted to follow him. Was she going to always feel this way with them?

Several hours later, Justin returned with a Diet Coke. He set it on a coaster on the desk before leaning against the side and smiling at her.

"Paul will be home in another thirty minutes. He's cooking tonight, so dinner will be a little later than last night. Thought the Diet Coke would tide you over."

She smiled up at him. She couldn't help it. "Thanks. I'll be fine 'til then."

"Ready to call it a day? I'm sure you're about sick of our style of filing by now."

She chuckled. "Well, it's interesting, but I think I've figured out your strange logic."

He eased closer to her and bent down to pick her up. "Grab your drink. Let's go watch the news while we're waiting on Paul."

Lana squealed when he lowered her enough to grab her drink. He carried her back to the living room and sat in one of the recliners with her on his lap. It felt good to be there. He switched the TV on and selected the news. She tried to remain still and not wiggle around as he absently rubbed his thumb back and forth over her thigh at the hem of her shorts. Just that little touch was playing havoc on her nerves.

The sound of the kitchen door slamming indicated that Paul was home. Her heart rate kicked up at the knowledge.

"We're in here, Paul." Justin squeezed her leg.

"Hey, babe. How are you feeling today?" Paul bent over and gave her a lingering kiss that left her aching for much more.

Damn Justin. He had shown her a little of what she had been missing all these years, and now she wanted it all. Working with them was going to be hell on her nerves.

"I'm fine." She quickly glanced back at the TV as heat climbed up her neck into her cheeks. He knew.

"Justin said you'd had a nice day today. Did you enjoy yourself?"

"I'm going to kill you," she mumbled at Justin.

Justin grinned and squeezed her thigh again. "We don't keep secrets, sweetheart. Just wait until after dinner. I bet Paul's going to try and find out for himself just how much fun you had."

Lana huffed out a breath and resisted the urge to bury her face in his shoulder. She might be a little naïve, but she didn't have to act like it. Instead, she refused to look at either of the two men and pretended to be interested in the TV.

"I'm going to work on dinner. How about chicken and rice, Lana?"

"Sounds good to me."

"Bring her into the kitchen so we can—play while I cook."

That caught her attention. She jerked her head up and saw the intent look on Paul's face. She could tell he had something planned, and she wasn't sure she was going to like it. Looking over at Justin, she caught him nodding at Paul. Damn, she was in trouble. They were up to something together.

Justin stood up with her in his arms. She tightened her grasp around his neck as he strode through the kitchen door behind Paul.

God, Paul looked good from behind. She couldn't take her eyes off of his ass. Evidently Justin noticed because he chuckled in her ear.

"Like what you see, honey? Paul will give you a show if you ask nicely."

She popped him on the top of the head. Paul did not need to hear that she'd been ogling him. He already thought highly of himself. Justin just chuckled and sat down at the table once they were in the kitchen.

"I need some inspiration for cooking tonight, Justin. It was damn hot out there." Paul washed his hands and turned around as he dried them.

"We can handle that, can't we, Lana." Justin began pulling off her shirt.

"Hey! What are you doing?" She slapped at his hands.

"Giving Paul some inspiration, sweetheart. Now be still. I don't want to hurt you by accident."

She closed her eyes while he pulled her shirt over her head and dropped it to the floor. Since she wasn't wearing a bra, her breasts were bare and open to Paul's view. The air-conditioning had the house nice and cool. It soon had her nipples standing at attention, or at least she told herself that was why they were pointed directly at Paul.

"Open your eyes, babe. I want to see you while Justin plays with them."

Paul wasn't smiling at her discomfort. He had a seriously aroused expression as he began gathering what he needed to cook.

Justin's big hands cupped her breasts as if offering them to Paul. Then he began pulling and pinching her nipples until she was so aroused, her head thrown back on his shoulder and her body arched so that her breasts pushed against his hands. He continued to play with her until she was sure she was going to come from that alone. As if knowing she was on the edge of flying, he nuzzled her neck and let go of her breasts.

"Oh, God. Why did you stop?"

"To move on to something else. Stand up."

Lana hesitated for just a second. She stared into Paul's eyes. His were heavy lidded, and there was a stillness about him that made her think he was waiting on her to move before he breathed again. She slowly slipped off of Justin's lap on her good leg and waited to see what Justin would do. She had a feeling she already knew.

Sure enough, he unfastened her shorts and slipped them down until they rested at her feet. She was trembling now as Paul's eyes grew even darker, if possible. He licked his lower lip as Justin helped her back on his lap where he separated her legs so that they were wrapped around the outside of his. He moved his legs apart, widening hers even more. Her wet pussy was spread wide to Paul's eyes.

"Beautiful." Paul continued working on dinner.

"Fuck, she's wet, Paul. Look at all that cream leaking from her hot cunt."

Paul's eyes seemed to focus on Justin's over her head for a few seconds then jerked back to her sopping-wet slit as his brother began circling her clit with his finger. She moaned and leaned back against Justin's chest as he teased her clit without touching it. Her eyes closed as arousal built inside of her.

"Open your eyes and look at me." Paul's voice sounded deeper, thicker.

She opened them and stared into Paul's but had to fight to keep them that way. All she wanted to do was grab Justin's hand and hold it against the clit so she could ride him to release. She couldn't ever remember being so horny and needy before in her life. She was reduced to chasing his finger with her hips, trying to force his finger where she wanted it.

"Be still." He popped the thigh of her good leg lightly before resuming his torturous attention to her pussy.

He ran his finger down her slit and then back up again. The more he teased her, the hotter she grew. Her body felt as if it were a living torch waiting on someone to take pity on her with a bucket of water.

"Please, Justin. Don't tease me."

"Shh, sweetheart. It will be so good when you come. Just hold on a little longer. See how hot you're making Paul. He's having trouble focusing on dinner."

"I can smell you from here, babe. Your scent is driving me fucking crazy."

Justin slipped a finger inside her pussy and swirled it around in her juices before pulling it back out and rubbing lightly over her aching clit. She squirmed and panted at the light touch, needing a much heavier one to come. Lana gave a frustrated growl when he lifted his finger away.

The sudden entrance of two fingers into her pussy had her gasping. Justin began pumping them in and out of her wet hole while whispering naughty suggestions in her ear just loud enough that Paul would be able to hear him. If she hadn't already been blushing all over, those dirty words would have colored her skin in no time. No one had ever said things like that to her before.

Her eyes darted back toward Paul and found his hands still as he watched in rapt attention Justin's fingers moving in and out of her cunt. Hidden behind the island, she couldn't see his crotch, but she imagined that his cock would be hard and poking out against the front of his jeans. She wanted to see the evidence of what she and Justin were doing to him. She wanted to know that his steady control had slipped and was all but lost as his brother tore away her last shred of resistance where they were concerned. He should have to suffer right along with her.

Chapter Thirteen

Paul couldn't take his eyes off where his brother's fingers were fucking Lana's pussy. The evidence of her arousal leaked down her pussy lips and coated Justin's hand as he pleasured her. His cock jerked at the little mewling sounds she made as she begged his brother for release.

Dinner totally forgotten now, Paul wiped his hands on a towel then adjusted his erection to take some of the pressure from the fucking zipper off of it. He walked around the island to lean his back against it so that he could see better. The more Justin pumped his fingers in and out of her hot, wet pussy, the harder his dick grew. Finally, he couldn't take it anymore, and he unfastened his jeans and pulled it out.

He noticed Lana's eyes grow impossibly wide as she watched him stroke himself. His cock jerked at the attention. When she licked her lips a moan escaped his lips. She was going to kill him with her sweet innocence. He was sure she was not a virgin, but it was obvious that she was unversed in so many things an experienced woman at home in her body would know. He itched to introduce her to the sensual delights he and Justin could show her. Unfortunately, she was injured and needed time to heal before they took things further with her.

Justin was killing him as he slowly worked his fingers in and out of her hot cunt. Lana couldn't be still, and she begged so prettily to come. He squeezed the base of his dick then ran his hand up and down, smoothing the drop of pre-cum over the bulbous head. It slicked his way as he slowly pumped his hand up and down. His balls hung taut and heavy between his legs. It wouldn't be long before they would draw up in preparation to shoot his load.

He continued to stroke himself as Justin changed tactics with Lana and curved his fingers up inside their woman. Paul knew he was rubbing over her sweet spot by the way she suddenly jerked in his brother's arms as her eyes rolled back. He increased the pressure around his dick in hopes he could stave off his own impending orgasm to coincide with hers.

"Hurry, Justin. I'm going to come."

Justin chuckled and dropped his other hand to play with Lana's clit.

"Oh, God! Please, oh, please, oh, please!"

"Ah, hell she's so fucking hot!" Paul felt his balls draw up and his cock begin to burn at the base as he began to lose his rhythm and his control.

Justin grinned across at him as he pinched Lana's swollen clit between his fingers as his other hand continued to stroke her G-spot. He leaned closer to her ear again and whispered in her ear while Paul struggled to walk across the short distance to stand in front of Lana's spread legs. His cock jerked in his hand as he began to shoot ribbons of cum across her breasts.

Lana screamed with her own climax, her head thrown back against Justin's shoulder as he drew out her release until she was gasping for breath. She trembled so hard he feared she would vibrate off of his brother's lap.

"God, you're amazing, baby." Paul lowered his head to hers and kissed her, reveling in her jerky gasps.

When he stood back up, Justin stood up with her in his arms. "I'm going to go get her cleaned up. We'll be back down to eat in a little while."

Paul just nodded. He was still too emotional from the experience to speak rationally. He trusted his brother to take care of her, and he needed to get himself back under control to finish dinner. She would be hungry after that. Fuck, he hadn't expected that to happen. Normally he was able to manage himself better than that. He wasn't used to losing his tight rein over his libido like that. It was Lana. She did it to him.

After washing up, Paul finished up the meal preparation and set the table for when they returned downstairs. He didn't have long to wait. Justin carried Lana back into the kitchen and settled her at the table. They made quick work of dinner, and while Justin cleaned up, Paul took over caring for their woman.

"How are you feeling?"

"Good. I'm not nearly as sore as I thought I would be. My leg is much better, too." She had her arms around his neck as he carried her into the living room.

She smiled shyly up at him as he relaxed into his recliner with her on his lap. It felt right having her there. Switching on the TV with the remote, he chose a channel with a popular drama show and waited as she slowly began to settle against him.

Justin joined them several minutes later in the other recliner. After the TV show was over, Paul noticed that Lana had fallen asleep. It was no wonder after having had an orgasm, a bath, and something to eat. Not to mention that she was still healing.

"She's sound asleep," he told his brother.

"Yeah. With everything that's happened to her the last few days, I'm not surprised. Besides, I doubt she ever gets a lot of rest between working two jobs. We'll make sure she gets plenty of rest from now on."

"There's so much about her that we don't know."

"I think she'll open up more with us now. We've gotten past her defenses. It's just a matter of time."

Paul looked down at Lana curled up on his lap. She seemed so peaceful right then. Normally her body remained stiff around them. He wanted her to always be relaxed in their presence. They would never hurt her. What would it take to totally break down her reserve?

She was so independent. They didn't want to break her or take away her spirit, but they wanted her to rely on them to take care of her. He needed to take care of her. It was who he was.

"She worked in the office some this afternoon before you got home. She's a regular whirlwind of activity. I watched to make sure she didn't overdo it or hurt herself, but she actually accomplished a lot, I think. At least you can see the top of the desk now." Justin chuckled quietly.

"I'd rather she just rest, but I guess that's too much to ask."

"She's going to need a stool to reach the top drawers in the filing cabinets and the bookshelves as well."

"I don't want her climbing, Justin."

"I'm not going to get her one until she's healed up." He frowned at Paul.

Paul sighed and realized he'd snapped at his brother. Lana had him tied up in knots. It wasn't like him to fuss with Justin. Normally they worked great together.

"I'm sorry. I know you wouldn't let her climb this soon. I'm just not used to feeling this way about someone. She has me aching to take her one minute and wanting to turn her over my knee the next."

Justin chuckled. "I know exactly what you mean. She's going to challenge us at every opportunity, Paul. She's used to taking care of herself, and letting us do that is going to go against everything inside of her."

"I know. We've got a long journey ahead of us, little brother."

"She's worth it, though."

Paul kissed the top of her head and breathed in her scent. She was worth anything he had to deal with to keep her in their lives. His need to control every aspect of her life would be the greatest challenge he'd ever faced, even over his time in the armed forces. No matter what the sacrifice, she was worth it. He'd do anything for Lana.

* * * *

Over the next several days, Lana worked in the office some and slowly made headway with learning their business. She managed to organize their chaos, and except for the top drawers of each of the file cabinets, she had them all straight and in order. Justin had promised that when she got the all clear from the doctor, he would get her a step stool for the office.

She would be going to get her stitches out of her head on Monday. She was looking forward to that. They had begun to itch, and she desperately wanted to take a shower and wash her hair for a change. As much as she enjoyed the long soaks in the massive tub in the master bathroom, she really wanted a hot shower.

"Hey, sweetheart. What are you thinking about over there?" Justin's warm voice brought a smile to her face.

"Just thinking that I get my stitches out on Monday and I'm excited. Plus, I'll be getting my stool for the office as well." She couldn't stop the smirk that crept across her face.

"Don't count your chickens before they're hatched. The doctor might not clear you for putting full weight on that leg yet."

"Spoilsport." She pouted.

Lana realized what she was doing and immediately wiped it off her face. She didn't flirt like this. That wasn't her, was it? So much had happened lately that she wasn't sure what she did anymore. She could feel her face heat at the memory of the night before when Paul had made her scream while he'd sucked and licked her pussy until she'd come. Justin had tortured her breasts and licked and kissed his way all over her body at the same time. No one had ever brought her to orgasm before and certainly never more than once in a night. Between Justin and Paul, she'd come three times last night. What would it be like when they finally made love to her?

"What are you thinking about over there? Your face is the prettiest color of pink I've ever seen."

She immediately turned away and concentrated on filing an invoice she'd uncovered filed in the wrong place earlier. No way was she going to admit that she fantasized about sex with them. Somehow she had to keep her wits about her. They weren't really serious. They were just playing with her. If they knew how much she wanted them, it would give them power over her. As much as she valued her independence, thoughts of being with them threatened to push her to give in. She squared her shoulders.

"Nothing. Explain how you work a job from start to finish so I can get a feel of how you operate your business."

"Changing the subject will work for a while, sweetheart, but not forever." He grinned at her then pulled his seat closer to the desk.

Lana had a pad and pencil ready to take notes. She needed a general idea of their work flow so she would know when something was missing or late.

"For a new account, we get a request for a quote. We schedule an appointment and go out to find out what they want and see what sort of problems there may be in giving it to them. We make a list out of materials needed and then the estimated man-hours and any special equipment we may need to rent. You would be responsible in getting us costs of the materials and such, as well as the labor costs. We'll show you how to figure all of that up, of course."

"Do you have set distributors you use or go with whoever you can get the best prices from?" Lana scribbled notes as they talked.

"We have a list of them we use and search for the best price. We'll get you that as well."

They discussed the business for another hour before Justin put a stop to it and hauled her off to the living room to wait for Paul to make it home. She found that she waited eagerly for whoever worked that day to make it back. She missed them and worried about the fact that they had managed to worm their way under her defenses. What was she going to do when she went back home?

"Have you heard from the sheriff again about my apartment? I really need to move back home. Someone is going to steal everything I have if I don't get that window fixed soon."

Justin jerked at the sudden change in the conversation. "What brought that up?"

"It doesn't matter. I need to get back to normal."

"Don't you like staying here? We've tried to make it nice for you."

"Justin, you and Paul have been more than nice to me. I really appreciate everything you've done for me, but I need to go home."

"I'll call the sheriff once Paul gets home and find out what is going on. Don't worry about the window. We've already had it replaced."

"Why didn't you tell me? How much was it?"

"Don't worry about it, Lana. It's taken care of."

"I have to repay you. I can't let you pay for my stuff. It's my responsibility."

"What's going on?" Paul walked in with a frown on his face.

Neither one of them had heard him when he'd entered the house. Lana guessed that proved how upset she was over finding out that they had gone behind her back to pay for having her window fixed. Now she wondered if they had been keeping anything else from her. Like the fact that her apartment had been released from the sheriff's department already.

"Why didn't you tell me about my window? Is my apartment ready for me to go back now? Or were you going to keep that a secret, too?"

"You don't need to go back there, baby. You have a home here with us." Paul walked over to stand in front of where she sat rigidly on the couch.

"I can't live with you two! I have my own place." Lana jumped up without paying any attention to her injured leg.

"That apartment is a fire trap waiting to happen."

"It's my home! You can't tell me where I can and can't live."

"Lana, that's no way to live. You deserve more than that." Justin spoke up once again.

"Now that I'm working for you, I'll be able to afford a better place. But that doesn't change the fact that it's time for me to go back home." She crossed her arms and glared at them.

Everything inside of her wanted to agree to stay with them, but she knew it was too dangerous. Given half a chance they would take over her entire life, and she'd never survive being controlled. Despite knowing they would never hurt her on purpose, their overbearing personalities would eventually choke her to death. Why did love have to be so complicated?

Love! What in the hell was she going to do? Admitting that she loved them both eased her aching heart, but her mind couldn't get around their demanding personalities. Lana had no choice but to leave if she was going to salvage any part of her sanity.

"We don't want you to go back there. It's too dangerous. Why don't you want to stay here with us?" Justin glanced over at Paul.

"Because it's not right. I shouldn't have stayed this long." Tears burned at the back of her eyes.

"You belong here with us, Lana. Don't push us away. I thought you were getting used to us." Paul stood in front of her with his hands in his pockets and a scowl on his face.

Strangely enough, she wasn't afraid of him. A little nervous, maybe, but she didn't fear him. They had been so good to her over the last few days. She purposefully didn't think about the nightly loving they treated her to. It was one of the reasons she knew she needed to leave. She was growing accustomed to having them take care of her. It had to stop. It was too late for her heart, she'd already lost it to them, but she could keep her pride intact by getting away from them now.

"I can't stay, Paul. It's not right. You want more from me than I can give."

"You mean more than you're willing to give." Justin spoke up again.

Lana looked over at him and felt her heart squeeze at the disappointment evident on his face. Did he really feel something for her, more than just lust? Her experience with men was almost nonexistent, but forever wasn't something she should expect from someone like them. They were out of her league. The sooner she realized that and moved on, the better. She just prayed she would be able to work with them and keep her job. Surely with them being out in the field most of the time they could work through any awkwardness that might arise.

"Please, Justin. Don't make this harder than it has to be. I'm not your type. In a few weeks or months, you'd get tired of me and then where would that leave me? I need to get on with my life. That means moving back to my place."

Justin stared at her for several seconds. Finally he stalked off. Paul's jaw clenched, and the muscles at the side of his face bunched and relaxed several times before he finally spoke.

"I'll check with Mac to see if it's okay for you to return yet. Before you spend another night there though, I'm going to make sure your locks are changed. If the doctor releases you on Monday, we'll move you back then." He jerked his hands out of his pockets and stalked off toward the kitchen.

Lana thought she would feel better knowing she would be going home soon, but instead she felt worse. Somehow the idea of returning to her lonely apartment didn't relax her like she thought it would. If anything, it seemed to stir up more feelings of restlessness than ever before. Her heart sank at the realization that she might be making a huge mistake.

Shaking it off, Lana collapsed back on the couch and fought back the tears that threatened to fall. Her heart might be lost, but she wouldn't let he pride go with it.

Chapter Fourteen

Sunday morning Paul stood on the back porch drinking his first cup of coffee while he waited for Justin to make it downstairs. He had no doubt that Lana would sleep for another couple of hours based on experience. He and Justin needed to talk. They were losing her, and that wasn't an option.

"Coffee is good." Justin closed the door behind him as he stepped out on the porch.

"She sleeping okay?"

Justin nodded and took a sip of the scalding liquid. "Checked on her before I came downstairs."

"I don't want her going back to that fucking apartment. It's a damn dump!"

"I don't either, but we can't keep her a prisoner here."

Paul ran a hand through his hair and leaned against the wooden post supporting the porch. He'd been over and over the problem in his head for the last few days and hadn't gotten any closer to a solution.

"If we try and force her to stay here, she's going to pull away. We've made too much headway to compromise it all now." Justin looked at him over the rim of the cup in his hand.

"Hell. Don't you think I know that? It doesn't make it any easier to watch her go back to that place."

"Our only option is to make her fall in love with us sooner rather than later. Somehow I don't see that happening in twenty-four hours. Let's plan to keep her busy at work as much as possible and follow her home each night to be sure she makes it in safe."

Paul scowled at his brother but had to admit that it was probably the best plan they would be able to come up with. Maybe if she spent enough time with them she would begin to fall in love and admit that they belonged together. In the meantime, he would have to curb his tendency to control everything and everyone around him. It wouldn't be an easy feat, but necessary to keep from scaring her off. Once she was theirs, he could relax and everything could go back to normal.

"Were you listening to anything I said?" Justin frowned at him.

"Sorry, I was thinking that the only option we had was to get her to fall in love with us."

"That's what I was saying. You're going to have to back off some, or you'll scare her off."

"She's not spooked that easily. She stands up to me when I try to make her take it easy."

Justin snickered. "She does at that. I like seeing her stand up to you. You can get out of hand sometimes."

"We've got to figure out how to ease her into being with us so that she doesn't feel pressured. She's a very independent woman who's used to taking care of herself. Hell, she took care of her mom for several years. Letting someone else do the caring for her isn't going to sit well with her."

"I think the first step in getting her to trust us more is to let her move back into that blasted apartment, but at the same time, court her. Make her feel special and treat her like a lady."

"I'm putting new locks on her door and bars on the fucking windows that she can unlock from the inside."

"That will take time to get ordered and installed," Justin pointed out.

"I already ordered them. They'll be installed some time on Monday." Paul smiled at his brother.

"Why didn't you tell me you already had it taken care of?"

"Because I was hoping you would be able to talk her into staying with us in the meantime. It didn't work." He winked at Justin. "Don't worry, you'll convince her soon enough. I have faith in you, little brother."

They both turned to go back inside when the back door opened and Lana peeked out. She looked charmingly disheveled despite having dressed in a sundress and sandals. Her long hair still looked mussed as if she'd raked her fingers through it and forgone a brush. He wanted to sit her down and brush her hair for her. He could almost feel the gentle tug as he drew it through her thick hair.

"Morning, sweetheart. How do you feel today?" Justin walked past her into the kitchen.

"Hmm. Okay, I guess. I couldn't sleep anymore. It's Sunday and I don't have to work, but I can't sleep in. I need to be doing something, or I'm going to get lazy."

Paul felt a small grin widen his mouth as he followed them inside. She was pouting, and she looked cute doing it.

"Baby, you don't have a lazy bone in your body. You could do with some time off to just laze around some. I bet you've never had a vacation in your life."

"Have you?" she asked with a smirk.

"She's got you there, Paul." Justin grinned across the room at him.

"Shut up. No one asked you anything." He scowled at Justin before turning back to Lana. "Are you hungry? What do you want for breakfast this morning?"

"I'm really not very hungry. I think I'll just eat a piece of toast with some jelly. What are your plans for today?"

Paul watched her as she prepared the bread for toasting. He could almost see the gears in her head turning as she thought. What was she thinking?

"I was thinking about watching some movies off of Netflix for a change. Got any requests?"

"Aw, man. Why did you ask her? She'll probably pick some chick flicks or girly movies like *Hope Floats*." Justin whined but didn't look nearly as worried as he let on.

Lana rose to take the bait. "I'll have you know I don't watch chick flicks. I like action movies or drama." She stuck her hands on her hips and frowned at Justin.

"Don't worry about him. He actually liked *Thelma & Louise*. After you finish eating we'll go browse through the new releases and pick out something to watch."

"There was action in *Thelma & Louise*. They drove off a cliff. Remember?"

Lana laughed at his obvious pout and patted him on the shoulder. Paul liked seeing her smile, and her laughter was addicting. He would never get enough of hearing it. Somehow they had to win her love. He couldn't fathom the idea of going on without her in their life. With the immediate threat of the killer gone, he could concentrate on winning her heart and cementing a place in her life for him and his brother.

* * * *

Lana argued playfully with Justin on movies until Paul put a stop to it and made the final decision. For the next hour and a half they watched the latest action-packed thriller complete with car chase scenes and gunfights. She found herself sitting between them as usual despite trying to settle in one of the recliners to put some distance between them.

She knew that tomorrow she would be moving back to her own place, and even though she knew it was the right thing to do, it didn't make it any easier to think about. Putting some space between them seemed like the best idea to her. Unfortunately, they weren't having any of it. Justin had promptly picked her up and plopped her back down between him and his brother on the couch.

Somehow she managed to survive the entire movie despite Justin's arm across her shoulders and Paul's hand on her knee. Thankfully there had been enough action to keep her attention focused on the movie instead of the heat of their skin seeping beneath her clothes. Mostly.

"Okay, the next movie will start in about thirty minutes. Time for everyone to run to the bathroom and get another drink." Justin jumped up and headed for the stairs.

"Wait! What did you pick?" She reached to grab the remote, but Paul beat her to it.

"You'll see when it starts." He actually winked at her. She'd never seen him wink before.

Exasperated, she stood up and hobbled to the downstairs bathroom then joined Justin in the kitchen to grab a Diet Coke. She glanced at the clock and sighed. It would be nearly one by the time the next movie was over. Her last day with them was slipping away. Despite knowing it was for the best, her emotions were conflicting, and she was afraid that if she studied them too deeply she wouldn't want to leave at all. Hell, she knew she didn't want to leave them. She loved them, but it didn't mean that it was right.

"Earth to Lana. Are you ready for the movie to start?" Justin's voice cut into her thoughts.

"Um, yeah." She settled down between them and waited to find out what they were watching.

It didn't take long for her to figure out they'd chosen one that had action, but also had a lot of *adult*-natured content as well. The idea of sitting between them while a couple on the screen had sex wasn't her idea of comfortable. She briefly considered escaping to the bathroom during one scene, but Justin paused the movie until she returned.

It felt as if the two men were closing in on her as she watched the movie. Even though she knew they hadn't moved any closer, it sure felt like they were smothering her. Her skin felt ultrasensitive, and her pussy grew wetter by the minute. She needed to change her panties by the time the movie was over with. Unfortunately, Justin had no intentions of letting her escape once the credits started scrolling down the screen.

"Hungry, Lana?"

"I sure as hell am even if she's not." Paul's growly voice had her jerking her head toward him.

He was leaning closer to her so that when she turned to face him, he was only a breath away from her lips. In a flash, he closed the gap and married his lips to hers. Then his hand cupped the back of her head and moved her where he wanted her. His tongue lapped at her lips until she opened to him and then stroked over hers. She had no control over her reaction or the way she returned the kiss. Where the brothers were concerned, she had no willpower to resist them.

His taste exploded across her tongue and drew a soft moan from deep in her throat. Heat built inside of her as the kiss took her places she didn't think she had any right to go. Longing for more had her hands grasping his shoulders, pulling him closer when she should have been pushing him away instead. How would she ever manage to live without them after having experienced so much of their sexual expertise over the last few days?

When Paul finally pulled away, she felt lost without him. Then Justin turned her toward him and resumed where Paul had left off. Once again she found herself on the receiving end of enough sexual lust to drown her. They were potent apart, but when Paul moved in behind her and began to feast on her neck, she lost all thoughts of resistance. She was theirs to do with as they pleased.

Please let them make love to me.

As if they heard her wordless pleading, Justin picked her up off the couch and carried her toward the stairs. She was so lost in the feeling of his arms around her that Lana didn't realize they were upstairs back in her room until Paul began pulling her clothes off of her. By that time, she had nothing on but her panties and Justin was totally nude.

"Shh, sweetheart. We'll take good care of you, just like we always do." He stroked her arms as he leaned her back and took possession of her lips once again.

Lana was distantly aware that Paul was undressing beside the bed as Justin devoured her mouth with lips that sipped at hers and teeth that nipped. His tongue soothed the tiny sting before exploring her mouth from top to bottom. Then Paul lay next to her and brushed aside her hair to nibble on her earlobe before sucking on it. He spread kisses down her neck and across her shoulder as Justin whispered naughty suggestions in her other ear.

"I'm going to lick that pretty pussy until you're screaming my name, Lana. Then I'm going to suck up all your sweet juice as you come."

"Oh, God, Justin."

"When he's finished eating you up. I'm going to fuck that hot cunt and make you come all over again. You're going to suck Justin's cock until he fills your throat with his cum." Paul's words in her other ear only added fuel to the fire already consuming her.

"Please!"

"What, baby? What do you need?" Paul asked between nips at her shoulder.

"Take me. I can't stand it." She thrashed between him and Justin.

Justin seemed to take her desperate pleading to heart. He slipped down the bed and nudged her legs apart with his broad shoulders. The feel of his skin against the inside of her bare thighs sent shivers down her spine. The first stroke of his tongue over her slit had her arching her back with desire.

Paul laid a hand over her pelvis and gently pressed her back to the bed. "Easy, baby. Let Justin have his fill of you. I'm going to taste these juicy nipples. I love how big they are."

The second his mouth closed over one tight peak she hissed out a breath. Then she was soaring once again as Justin picked that moment to spread her pussy lips and attack her opening with his tongue in earnest. He circled her clit until she knew it was poking out from its hood for a better chance at being discovered. The tease didn't pay any attention, though. Instead, he lapped at the juices beginning to coat her legs as she felt her pulse speed up.

His brother had a hand on her other nipple now, twisting and pinching it as he nipped and drew in on the first one. She could feel the suction of his mouth tight against her breast, hot and relentless. The tingling grew sharper and traveled down that invisible line to her clit. Having pleasured her so many times before now, they knew what it took to get her juices flowing and could draw out the feeling forever.

Justin chose that moment to plunge a finger inside of her cunt as he lapped lightly over her clit, giving her just enough touch to ramp up the need building inside her. She whimpered as he added a finger and began to fuck her with them.

Paul changed breasts and the loss of his heated mouth on the first nipple allowed the cool air to tease it as he took in as much of her other breast as possible. When he backed off of it to settle for just the elongated nipple, Lana grabbed hold of his head and held it against her there. She didn't want to lose him from that side as she had the other. He chuckled against her, sending chills along her arms.

The sudden swipe of Justin's fingers against her hot spot had her fighting Paul's hand on her abdomen as she bucked with the thrilling sensation those evil fingers produced. Over and over he stroked the spongy skin then pressed on it as he sucked hard on her clit while his brother pinched and pulled on her nipples with both sets of fingers. Paul took her scream into his mouth as he kissed her. Justin growled against her sensitive flesh while she came apart in their arms.

No sooner had she begun to settle than the brothers had changed places, with Paul sheathing his cock and pressing against her opening as Justin aimed his cock at her mouth. Lana opened her mouth, eager for a taste of him. As soon as she was able to reach him with her tongue, she licked across the top of the mushroom crown, drawing out a drop of pre-cum. It exploded across her taste buds like a fine wine.

Justin hissed out and dug a hand in her hair at the scalp. His cock jerked in her mouth, and she quickly sucked on it to keep from losing it.

The pressure of Paul against her slit briefly drew her attention to him as he pressed his way inside of her.

"Fuck! You're so tight. I'm never going to last." The strained words didn't sound like they came from his throat.

He pulled out and then pushed back in, gaining more ground with the short thrust. Lana couldn't help moaning around Justin's dick as she sucked more of it inside her mouth. He tightened his hold on her head. She thrilled at the rawness of it. Knowing that he was on the edge of control because his cock was in her mouth gave her enough confidence to take more of him. She ran her tongue all along the length of him and paid special attention to the notch beneath the crown.

"Your mouth feels so good, so hot and tight. Take it all, sweetheart. I know you can. Just relax your throat and let me in." He pushed deeper into her. "God, yes! Just like that."

Lana followed his directions and relaxed as he slipped deeper into her throat. She struggled to breathe through her nose and not gag.

Paul's sudden plunge deep into her cunt drew a scream from her throat that vibrated across Justin's cock. He groaned as she fought to adjust to the length and breadth of Paul's invasion. She'd never taken anyone as large as he and Justin were. Her previous lovers, all two of them, had been less endowed. The feeling of fullness seemed to be more noticeable with one in her mouth while the other cock was reaching for his brother from below.

Her pussy stretched around him as he pulled back and plunged in once again. Despite the condom, she could feel every bump and vein forging its way inside of her. His balls bounced against her ass when he sank his thick length all the way inside her. There was nothing she could do except accept him as he tunneled in and out of her wet cunt.

Justin's strokes in and out of her mouth began to falter as he groaned and dug his nails into her scalp. She reached between his legs and fondled the wrinkly sac holding his balls. They felt heavy in her hand. Even as she thought that, they began to draw up tighter against his body.

"I'm gonna come, Lana. Take me all. Swallow my cum."

His raspy voice tightened things deep inside her, knowing that she was causing him to lose control. The power of it sang along her veins even as he began to fill her mouth and throat with thick spurts of his semen. She struggled to swallow it all then licked him clean and wiped the last little bit off her lips with her tongue. He collapsed next to her after withdrawing his softening cock from her mouth. He kissed her despite her having just swallowed his cum.

"You're fucking amazing, woman." He kissed her cheek then wrapped one hand over a breast as he struggled to regain his breathing lying next to her on the bed.

Chapter Fifteen

Lana reveled in the aftermath of Justin's climax. His hot breath fanned against her cheek and in her ear as he tunneled one arm beneath her neck and played with her nipple with his free hand. The overwhelming power she felt from sucking his cock did nothing to temper the heat building in her bloodstream with Paul's cock deep in her cunt. Instead it sharpened the sensation of his thick dick rasping over sensitive tissue, sending sizzling licks of flames all along her body.

"She's squeezing my cock like a fucking vise. Justin, man. I can't last." The strain in his voice told her that he was close even if she hadn't heard the words.

Justin moved slightly and his hand slipped down between them to slide around her clit even as his mouth latched on to her nipple. The dual sensations along with the glide of Paul's cock across her sweet spot soon had her body shaking in desperate need. The pressure inside of her built until she thought she would die from it.

Paul pounded in and out of her body, his fingers digging into her hips as he seemed to race to the end. Still, despite all the pleasure they had given her and the unending spiral of aching need building in every nerve ending, nothing could have prepared her for the detonation at her center when Justin bit her nipple and pinched her clit at the same time.

A river of heat burned its way through her veins as lights exploded behind her eyelids. Then pleasure unlike anything she had ever felt before consumed her alive. Somewhere in all of the mind-blowing experience she felt Paul's climax as he spilled his seed deep inside of her. The roaring in her ears deafened her to anything else for brief moments after that. Blind and deaf, Lana fought the pleasure even as she welcomed it on another level. It slowly receded, leaving her paralyzed and emotionally raw.

She knew that the reason it had been so heart-stopping perfect was because she loved them. Nothing had prepared her for how much of her soul she would lose with the explosion. Already the knowledge that she would never be able to hold them poked at her. She brushed it aside to worry about later. For now, she wanted to bask in the afterglow of their lovemaking. There was no way she would ever admit that it had been nothing but sex for anyone but her.

Dimly she became aware of Justin whispering how good she was and how sexy she looked while Paul kissed his way up her abdomen to her breasts before collapsing to the side. She hadn't even felt it when he'd pulled from her. Somehow she was glad she had missed that inevitable loss.

"Hell! I'm done for. Lana, you wasted me, baby."

She felt the prickle of tears in the back of her eyes and struggled to keep them from falling. She didn't want them to ask questions. Instead, she started to get up to escape into the bathroom, but Justin stopped her.

"Whoa, darling. I'm going to run you some bathwater so you can relax. I'll be right back."

Justin's fingers absently ran up and down her arm, but he didn't hug her or say anything more than he'd already said. She wasn't sure what she expected, but for some reason, his silence cemented her need to move out. She knew it hadn't meant anything to him like it had to her. They would be used to meaningless sex. After all, they were Greek gods when it came to their bodies. The fact that they knew their way around a woman's body only proved it.

Despite warning herself not to get involved with them, she'd done it. Then when she'd vowed not to fall in love with them, she'd done that as well. Now she felt as if she had a connection to them, and when it broke, it could very well kill her.

"Okay, sweetheart. I've got your water ready." Justin picked her up despite her assurance that she could walk. "I like carrying you."

He carefully stood her up in the tub, and then helped her kneel in the water. The warmth soon relaxed her muscles that had begun to tense up with worry. She refused to let her mind completely ruin her mood. Instead, she would go with whatever the men did for this last day and night. Tomorrow was soon enough to deal with the aftermath of the situation. She would build up her defenses once everything was settled and she was back in her own apartment.

After what felt like only a few minutes, Paul roused her and helped her out of the tub. He toweled her dry then helped her back into the bedroom. Justin was nowhere to be seen. As she pulled on clothes, Paul watched her through heavy-lidded eyes.

"What are you thinking?" Lana couldn't stop the question from coming out of her mouth.

"Remembering how you looked when you came earlier. You're beautiful when you climax. I loved watching it even though I was almost out of it with my own. Next time, I'm just watching while Justin fills you with his cock."

She didn't tell him that there wouldn't be a next time because she honestly wanted there to be one, maybe even tonight. She couldn't say anything though and changed the subject to one she felt more at ease with.

"Where's Justin?"

Amusement filled his eyes. "He's downstairs making sandwiches. It's nearly four."

Panic that the day was almost gone threatened to release the tears still hovering near the surface. Despite it having been hours since her meager breakfast of toast and jelly, Lana wasn't sure she could eat anything.

Paul took her hand once she'd finished dressing and led her down the stairs. When they entered the kitchen, Justin had a plate of sandwiches piled high and the table set for them. While the men consumed theirs, Lana managed only a few bites before she gave up and drained her glass. She avoided looking at either man in hopes they wouldn't notice her lack of appetite.

To her relief, they didn't broach the subject. Instead, they quickly cleaned up and escorted her back to the living room where Paul pulled her onto his lap in the recliner while Justin selected another movie to watch.

"How about a comedy?" Justin scrolled through the offerings on the screen.

"That sounds like a good idea." Paul stroked her arms with the palms of his hands.

Lana didn't bother answering. She was much too aware of Paul's muscular frame and the rock-hard cock pressing against her ass to offer a coherent answer. Each movement of his chest as he drew in a breath reminded her of his wide chest and broad shoulders. Though he was tender when stroking her arms, she could easily imagine those hands bunched tightly into a fist when angry. She knew he would never hurt her, but there was no doubt that he had the strength to hurt someone if he chose to.

"Lana? Are you asleep, baby?" Paul's whispered words finally broke through her thoughts.

"No, sorry. I guess I wasn't paying attention."

"Thinking about anything in particular?"

"Just thinking about what all I need to do tomorrow to get ready for work next week."

She felt him stiffen and heard the sigh even as the movie started, drowning out any hopes of further conversation. She was relieved to be let off the hook for now. Settling back, Lana tried to relax enough to follow the movie.

Two hours later, Justin stood up and stretched, laughing about the way the movie had ended.

The ringing of a phone nearby jarred her as Paul shuffled her over to one side so he could retrieve his cell. Justin leaned over and plucked her from his brother's lap as Paul answered.

"Let's go fix a snack before time for bed. I know you need to get rested for the rest of the week."

"Put me down, Justin. I need to walk or I'm going to be too stiff to when I'm actually by myself and have to do it."

Although it was obvious by his expression that he didn't want to do it, Justin allowed her to slide from his arms and stand on her own. She held on to his arm until she was sure she had her balance. Then she led the way into the kitchen as Paul continued talking to someone in the background. Evidently there was a problem somewhere he needed to work out. It seemed to her they could have waited until Monday morning to call him instead of bothering him on a weekend.

"Do you always get phone calls on the weekend about work?"

Justin looked up from where he had been bent over exploring the contents of the fridge. She couldn't help but admire the way his jeans flattered his muscular ass or the way they showcased his tight thighs. She had to stop herself before she drooled like a sex-starved teenager.

"Sometimes, but not often, thank goodness."

"Seems like it should be able to wait a few more hours until Monday."

"Usually it can, but occasionally there are emergencies in this business. Like when there is a water line busted in a sprinkler system or if a car ran up into someone's yard and damaged it."

"I suppose if you want to keep a good business name you have to handle those types of things as soon as possible."

Justin pulled out some fruit and began cutting it up on a plate. Once he'd finished that, he located some cheese and sliced it as well. Lana searched for crackers and lined the plates with them.

"Even when they know we can't do anything until the next day, they feel like they've solved a part of their problems by letting us know right away. It helps to calm them down when they are panicking, and that puts us in a good light with them."

"Customer satisfaction."

"Precisely." Justin stopped and kissed her nose.

Paul joined them in the kitchen once again and arched an eyebrow at the food on the bar.

"Looks like someone is hungry again."

Lana blushed as she bit off a piece of pineapple.

"She didn't eat much at lunch. Not that I blame her. My sandwiches weren't very appetizing."

"Oh, it wasn't that. They were fine. I just wasn't hungry for some reason." Ashamed that she had made him think she hadn't liked his efforts, Lana quickly stabbed another piece of fruit with her fork.

Justin took the fork away from her and fed the slice of fruit to her by hand. The heat in his eyes when she licked the juice off her lips sent butterflies fluttering around in her belly. Paul snagged her attention when he offered her a piece of cheese on a cracker. She opened her mouth and took a bite. He leaned over and licked the crumbs from her lips. Another jolt of awareness shot through her, sending shivers down her spine.

They took turns feeding her by hand until she couldn't eat anymore. Then they ate while sending smoldering looks her way and continually touching her on the arms, at her waist, and across her shoulders.

While the men cleaned up, Lana made a quick escape and hurried up to the bedroom where she stripped from her clothes and pulled on her pajamas, getting ready for bed. By the time Justin and Paul had made it upstairs, she was burrowed beneath the sheet, trying to calm her speeding heartbeat and shaking limbs. Part of her hoped they would sleep in their own beds that night to keep temptation out of reach, but part of her prayed they would stay with her so she had one last night to feel safe and wanted between them.

The bedroom door opened and both men stalked into the room, pulling off clothes and tossing them aside as they approached the bed. In that moment, she had no doubt they planned to ravish her, and Lana was completely on board with the idea.

When they crowded up next to her and took turns kissing her gently on the lips, she expected them to take it further. The fact that they didn't tore another little piece of her heart. Paul kissed her temple then turned over and faced the edge of the bed. There was no way she would beg them to make love to her when they obviously didn't want to. She turned as well to face Paul's back and tried to make herself fall asleep. Unfortunately, there was no way she would be able to when her heart was bleeding and her feelings had been tromped on by the two men in bed with her. Hearing their snores only made it worse.

Lana thought back over everything that had happened over the last week and decided that they had lost interest in her, but still felt responsible for her since she was in their home and going to be working for them. There was no doubt that they needed help with their business in the office setting, so she knew it wasn't a job made just for her. Still, now that she'd slept with them, they were tired of her. It would be up to her to pretend that none of it mattered and keep things on a business level from here on out.

Somehow she had to convince her heart that it wasn't broken and that she didn't need them to survive day in and day out. This job was paramount in her being able to move out of the dump she was living in and begin to build a new life for herself. She would not screw it up by becoming a simpering idiot hanging on to them like a leech. She had more pride than that.

"What are you thinking so hard about over there?" Justin's voice startled her.

"N–nothing. I was just going over some things about the office in my head."

He was quiet for so long that Lana thought he'd fallen back asleep. When he spoke again, she heard something strained in his voice.

"Somehow I don't think that was the entire truth, sweetheart. Get some sleep. We'll talk more in the morning."

Lana felt him nuzzle his face into the back of her neck before he sighed and turned over. Tears slipped from her eyes and wet her cheeks. Come morning, she vowed that she would have better control over her emotions. Come morning, she would be a professional and everything would go back to normal.

Chapter Sixteen

As soon as the men had gotten up Monday morning, Lana slipped out of bed and took a quick shower and dressed for her trip to the doctor. Then she made sure she had everything packed and sitting by the door so that they could easily carry it all downstairs to load in the truck. They ate a quick breakfast then Justin and Paul loaded the truck, putting all of her things in the back seat rather than in the bed of the truck. This meant she was stuck sitting between them in the front.

Justin held her hand as the doctor removed the stitches from her head and checked her wounds before giving her the all clear.

"You healed up nicely. There won't even be much of a scar, and it will be hidden by your bangs. If you're self-conscious about that one or the one on your thigh, you can get something over the counter at the drugstore to help fade it."

She thanked the doctor, but wasn't worried about the tiny scars. It wasn't like she was a beauty queen needing to defend her crown or anything, and Lana had never been vain about her looks.

The men ushered her out of the doctor's office and back into the truck. They stopped at the Riverbend Diner and had a quick lunch before Paul finally headed toward her apartment. She felt as if they had been postponing the inevitable for some reason. Once they pulled into the parking lot and she saw the custom security doors and windows truck in the lot, Lana knew what they had been doing.

"What have you done?" She stared at Paul.

"Why do you assume I've done anything? It could have been Justin."

"Justin would have put new locks on the door, but you don't do anything as predictable as changing the locks. You have to change the entire fucking door!"

"Calm down, Lana. I didn't put up a security door like I wanted to. I had them put up reinforced locks and dead bolts and put up security bars on the windows. You can unlock them from inside if you need out for a fire. Merely changing the locks on the door wouldn't have done a damn bit of good when the bastard went through the window like he did."

Lana swallowed around the lump in her throat at that reminder. Still, she couldn't allow them to just take over her life like they were. Like Paul was. The jury was still out on Justin.

"I want a bill so I can pay you back." She stubbornly crossed her arms and glared straight ahead.

"You don't have to pay me back. The apartment owner knows his apartments aren't up to code in a lot of areas and agreed to accept their installation as your rent for the next two months. You don't owe us anything." His knuckles had turned white as he gripped the steering wheel tightly enough she was afraid he would bend it.

Justin muttered something under his breath and opened the door to get out. He helped her with her seat belt then lifted her off the seat and set her down outside the truck. He took her hand and led her toward the apartments. She heard Paul behind them as they walked up the sidewalk toward her door.

"We'll look around and be sure it's clean and safe before we unload your things." Justin walked up to the man working on the door to her apartment. "Hey, Vance. Thanks for getting to this so quickly."

The other man grinned, shifting the screwdriver to his other hand, and shook Justin's hand before stepping forward to shake Paul's as well.

"Glad to help. We got both of the windows installed without any trouble and they work smooth as silk. I'm just adjusting the dead bolt so it's not so stiff. I'll have the keys for you in a few minutes."

"We're going to go inside and be sure everything is okay to move her back in." Justin nodded at the other man and stepped inside the building.

Lana wanted to pull free of his hand because it was doing a number on her ability to think straight and remain resistant to the pull he had over her. When she looked over her shoulder, it was to see Paul still talking to Vance.

"Let's check out your bedroom first. The key to the window is in the lock right now, but I want you to keep it on the bedside table so you are able to get to it, but an intruder can't reach it through the bars if he breaks the window."

She nodded and let him show her how to work the lock on the window and open the bars to escape in case of a fire. Then she pulled the key from the lock and placed it on her bedside table. She looked over the room and realized someone had cleaned it and her mattress had been replaced. She didn't broach the subject with Justin because she was secretly relieved not to have to deal with the blood stains on the sheets and mattress. Just thinking about it had the newly healed wounds on her belly itching.

Justin seemed to realize what she was thinking about because he wrapped her in his arms and turned her away from the bed to check the rest of the tiny room.

"Is everything like you want it?"

"Yes, thank you for having it cleaned for me. I don't think I would have been able to handle coming back to deal with the mess."

Paul walked in. She turned to him and licked her lips. His eyes followed the movement, making it hard to think for a second.

"I really do appreciate everything you've done for me. I don't mean to sound ungrateful. I'm just used to handling things myself, and you both tend to go a bit overboard with it all."

"We only want what is best for you, baby. Your safety is very important to us. If we go a little overboard it's because we care about you so much. I wish you could accept that."

Lana took a step closer to him and reached out to smooth a hand down his shirt. Just that simple touch sent shock waves through her body. Everything about the two men not only turned her on, but settled her to some degree as well. She knew that if circumstances had been different, she would have hung on to them with both hands.

Paul covered her hand with his and stared down into her eyes as if he could read her thoughts. She shifted uncomfortably from one foot to the other before gently pulling from his grasp. Then she turned toward Justin and smiled.

"I guess we can unload my things now. I need to get everything put away so I can get some rest before work tomorrow. I hear my new bosses are slave drivers."

Justin grinned and urged her through the door and back into the living area. He settled her on the loveseat. Vance walked up and handed him several keys.

"Everything is done. The keys all fit and work smoothly. The locks all work on the same key. If you need anything else or if there's a problem, call me. I'll get right over." Vance smiled at her and followed Justin and Paul back outside.

A few minutes later, the men returned carrying some of her things. When she would have gotten up to follow them into her bedroom, Justin shook his head and told her to wait until they had everything inside. She figured it was a good idea since the apartment was so small and they were two very large men. Getting around would be an issue if she was trying to unpack as they added more stuff.

Once they had made the last trip, Lana joined them in the bedroom. She wasn't sure what to say to them. Paul looked around the room with an unreadable expression on his face. Justin just sighed.

"Need some help unpacking, sweetheart?"

"Thanks, but I can manage better on my own. I know where everything goes and you don't. I really appreciate…"

"Don't thank us again, Lana." Paul's clipped statement had her biting her tongue.

"We'll let you get busy so you can rest. Don't overdo it. We want you rested and happy tomorrow." Justin smoothed over Paul's abrupt words.

"Well, okay. I'll see you out." She held out her hand for the keys and noticed that Justin only handed her two. They each kept a copy for themselves.

Deciding not to push the subject, Lana followed them to the door. Justin pulled her into his arms and kissed her. His lips brushed lightly against hers then pressed harder to gain entry into her mouth. She opened easily to his. Her hands rested against the top of his shoulders and she had to resist the urge to curl them around the back of his neck. Then Paul was pulling her from his arms into his. He crushed her lips against his before stabbing his tongue insistently into her mouth. She couldn't resist his taste or the way he dominated the kiss. They were so different in how they approached everything, from their kisses to their styles of lovemaking.

When Paul released her, he looked as if he wanted to say something, but he just turned away and walked through the door. Justin touched her cheek with a soft smile.

"Lock up, Lana. We'll see you in the morning. Don't bother knocking. Just come on in. You know where everything is."

"Goodnight, Justin." She watched him walk out to the parking lot, but closed and locked the door when he shook a finger at her.

It took her nearly two hours to put away everything they had taken to their house for her. She was thankful that someone had stocked her refrigerator with milk, eggs, cheese, and orange juice. She also had some fresh fruit and bread. After a light meal of cheese and crackers with an apple, Lana sat down to evaluate her finances and how she would rearrange her budget.

By the time bedtime rolled around, she had figured out how to get her debts paid off faster and still manage to move to a nicer apartment within the next six months. She would save for her deposits and start looking right away. Sometimes there was a waiting list and she didn't want to lose out on a nicer, safer place. Now all she had to do was manage to work with Justin and Paul without making a fool of herself around them.

Hopefully they would remain out on jobs the majority of the time and she would be by herself and not have to deal with being around them so much. Still, it wouldn't be easy keeping her feelings under lock and key when they were near. She had no doubt they wanted their sexual relationship to continue, but she had to put a stop to it or she wouldn't be able to continue to work for them when they finally broke it off. Already the idea of never feeling their arms around her as they filled her body tightened the band around her heart. Lana wiped away the tears that snuck up on her and refused to think about it any further. It was time for a bath and then bed. This was the start of a new life for her, and she would be damned if she fucked it up because she wanted something she couldn't have.

* * * *

Early the next morning, Lana dressed and drove to her new job. She let herself in through the front door since it was closest to the office. Since she parked out front, she didn't really even know if the guys were still at home or if they had already left for the day. It didn't really matter as far as her job duties went, so she settled in and began organizing her day.

A little after eight the phone began ringing and between filing, filling out orders, and answering the phone, Lana didn't slow down until nearly one. Lunch was to be a peanut butter and jelly sandwich she had brought with her. She knew there were Diet Cokes in the fridge in the kitchen, so she took her sandwich with her and ate on the island. No sooner had she taken her first bite than the back door opened and both Paul and Justin stepped into the kitchen. She couldn't help but notice that their eyes lit up when they spotted her.

"Hey there, sweetheart. How are you feeling today?" Justin leaned over and kissed her on the nose before following Paul to wash up at the sink.

"I'm doing just fine. Staying busy. The phone has been ringing off the hook. I have quite a few messages for you. None were serious, so I didn't bother you with them while you were out."

"That's fine. Unless there's a problem, it can wait until we check in with you." Paul grabbed a loaf of bread and some things from the refrigerator to make sandwiches.

Justin took a stool next to her and bumped shoulders with her. "Missed you today. Got used to being home with you."

"Got lazy, huh?" She grinned at him.

Paul chuckled. "Yeah, you could say that. He whined all morning about checking on you."

"Hey, it was her first day and we just left her to sink or swim."

"Well, officially maybe, but I actually started last week, so it wasn't a big deal at all."

Paul handed over a couple of sandwiches to Justin and everyone settled down to eat in silence. Lana was glad that it was a comfortable silence. She didn't feel like making small talk, and it wasn't expected of her. She figured once they were through, they would want to go over the messages. She also had a couple of questions on some invoices that needed filing.

If things continued like this, she would be okay dealing with her feelings about them and the job. As long as they didn't push her, everything would work out for the best in the long run.

"When you're ready, I'll be in the office and we can go over your messages." Lana stood up and cleaned off her spot.

"We'll be in there in a couple of minutes." Paul crumpled his napkin and picked up the glass of tea he was drinking.

By the time she had gotten settled and answered the phone again, the men walked into the office and took up residence on the corners of the desk. Justin leaned over her while she took a message and ran his fingers up and down her arm. She tried to glare at him but wasn't sure if it came out that way or not. So much for an easy, professional relationship. He had already set the stage for how things would be.

"Here are the messages. If you have any questions, I think I can remember them all fairly easily." She handed over the small stack to Paul as soon as she got off the phone.

Paul divided them up and handed some to Justin. She busied herself entering information on the computer while they mumbled between themselves on things. Then Paul reached over and dropped two on the blotter in front of her.

"Those two you can call back and tell them both that we'll contact them next month when we have an opening. Put the notes in the file for August. I'll handle these others and let you know if you need to do anything with them later."

Justin handed her three slips for the August file and kept the rest. "Good notes. I know exactly what they want without having to sound clueless when I call them back."

Lana couldn't help but bask in the praise. She turned and dropped the papers into the August file in one of the cabinets. When she turned back around it was to find Paul standing in front of her between her and the desk. His eyes promised all sorts of bad things. Things she would love to experience, but she had promised herself to make this into a professional-only relationship.

When he backed her up against the filing cabinets, she gasped at the sudden impact. He dropped his hands to her shoulders and pulled her toward him. There was no ignoring the hard ridge of his cock pressing at her belly, nor was there any way to avoid the temptation of his lips as they closed over hers in a heated exchange. Tiny electrical impulses fired along her nerve endings as he deepened the kiss until she was digging her fingers into the muscles of his arms as they held her.

All of her well-intentioned plans to remain immune to their advances melted in the heat of that kiss. God, was that her whimpering as he ate at her mouth? She needed to stop him. She needed him to take all of her.

Then Justin eased between her and the filing cabinet. He braced her against his hard chest and equally hard dick. The thickness of him rested between the cheeks of her ass. It drew another moan from her mouth that was swallowed up by Paul. Justin's hands smoothed up and down her arms before he moved her hair to one side, baring her neck. She shivered when his moist lips rested there just below her ear.

"God, you taste amazing." He nipped then sucked in her earlobe.

One of Paul's hands slipped beneath her shirt to rest against the bare skin of her waist. It wasn't exactly where she wanted it, but it was a start. She whimpered around Paul's kiss, hoping he would move his hand higher to her breast. Where had her resolve gone?

"You're wearing too many clothes, sweetheart." Justin nipped once more at her neck before running his hands under her shirt and helping his brother pull it over her head.

"But we're in the office." She pulled back from Paul and stared up into his face.

"And I'm going to bend you over that desk and fuck your brains out in about two minutes."

"Hell, yeah!" Justin ran his callused hands up her torso before unhooking her bra so that his brother could pull it off of her.

"This isn't a good idea, guys." Her head agreed, but her body was on board with Paul and Justin.

"It's a great idea. Now bend over the desk for us, babe."

Lana slipped from between them and bent over the desk so that her ass was in the air and her hands were braced shoulder width against the desktop. It didn't surprise her when one of the men reached around her to unfasten her slacks and slip them down her legs. Next dropped her panties. They steadied her so she could step out of them.

"Fuck, I love to see you naked. All that creamy flesh just asking for me to lick you all over." Justin's voice came from her left side.

She turned, and he immediately captured her lips in a searing kiss. Even as he explored her mouth with his tongue, Paul was exploring her breasts with his fingers, pinching and twisting her nipples. The dual sensations overwhelmed her good sense, and all thoughts of why this would never work flew out the window.

Paul seemed to push Justin off to one side, because suddenly his body covered hers from behind, and he was fiddling with the zipper of his jeans.

"You're ours, Lana. We'll never let you go."

Chapter Seventeen

Paul's words slammed into her head and heart as he released his cock and filled her aching cunt with the hard length of him. *No, no, no. He didn't really mean that.* She tried to reason with herself that he was just saying it in the heat of the moment. She couldn't allow those words to take root inside of her or she would go crazy when they grew tired of her.

She moaned as Paul's rough hands held tightly to her hips while he filled her pussy over and over again. He seemed to be hell-bent on claiming her as he pounded her body against the desk. The sounds of flesh meeting flesh filled the room.

"Aw, hell. Look at you, Lana. Your face is flushed and you have the prettiest expression on your face. Watching my brother's dick sliding in and out of your sweet pussy is driving me crazy."

Lana's climax grew out of nowhere as Justin's naughty words drove her excitement higher. The feel of Paul's thick cock tunneling in and out of her wet hole sent tingling vibrations all along her slit. The bump of his heavy balls against her clit kept it primed and ready for just the right touch.

"Fuck, I'm not going to last. Your hot cunt has my dick wrapped up in wet velvet." Paul slipped one hand under her and located her clit.

Stars exploded behind her eyes when he began to rub over the tight bundle of nerves with his finger. Little warning bells began to peal in her ears as her orgasm overtook her and carried her out to sea. The long, strong tide moved her along until nothing made sense but

Paul's cock emptying his cum deep inside of her and the feel of his hands on her flesh.

No sooner had he finished than Justin was pulling him off of her and taking his place. She gasped for breath as he slid deep inside of her in one long push. His guttural growl told her he enjoyed it even as he stilled deep inside of her.

"God, I missed your sweet pussy."

"It hasn't been that long, Justin." Lana had to fight around her ebbing climax to speak.

"It was still too long." He pulled out and slammed back into her quivering cunt once more.

All she could think about was that it would never last and she wanted it to so desperately. Why couldn't they fall in love with her? *Because you aren't good enough for them. They're out of your league, Lana.*

Justin pulled almost all the way out once again, but this time, he fed his cock to her slowly until he was resting lightly next to her cervix. She felt his hand press at her back, forcing her to rest her face against the cool desk. At this angle, he had more room to spear her flesh with his thick dick. The sensation of wet flesh being dragged over sensitive nerve endings awakened her sweet spot even more. Each rasp over the spongy tissue had her writhing over the desk.

"Come for me, Lana. I'm not going to be able to hold on. It's too good." Justin's strained voice was all the additional stimulation she needed.

Fire burst from her G-spot up to her clit. The surges of destruction spread out through her womb and attacked her body as she came in hard waves. The hot spurt of Justin's seed inside of her spurred another small climax that left her gasping for breath. Justin's hot body rested against her back, and she realized he hadn't gotten undressed all the way. She was totally nude, and the two men had only lowered their jeans to fuck her.

"Aw, hell!" Justin's loud curse startled her.

"What is it?"

"Paul, we didn't use condoms, man. What were we thinking?" He gently pulled out of her and kissed her back. "I'm sorry, Lana. We're clean, but it's no excuse for forgetting."

She slowly stood up, grasping the chair for balance after having been horizontal over the desk. She felt the combination of their seed and her juices leak down her legs.

"It's all right. I'm on the pill. I'm clean, too. It's been a long time for me." She hated admitting that but figured they already knew that.

Paul walked back into the room with a washcloth. She hadn't even realized he'd left the room. When he knelt on the floor and began to clean her, Lana felt embarrassed and tried to take the cloth from him.

"I can do that." He slapped her hands away.

"Don't, babe. I've got you. Stand still."

Justin kissed her forehead and rested his chin on top of her head. "We've got to go back to the job site, but I don't want to leave you."

Paul stood up and leaned into her from behind. "Neither do I. Be here when we get home tonight, Lana."

"I'll think about it. I really need to get back to work now. You need to answer your messages." She pulled away from them and began dressing without looking at them.

She didn't know how to handle the emotions swirling around inside of her. Part of her wanted to give in and see where they would take her, while another part of her feared losing what she had fought so hard to hold on to. Her sense of self and being able to take care of herself were important to her. But for some reason, when they were near her, she lost sight of all of that. If only she could believe they wouldn't lose interest in her eventually.

Tension-filled silence stretched as she fiddled with her clothes before turning back around. Both men stared at her with serious expressions.

"What?"

"Why are you pulling away from us again?" Justin asked.

"You start closing yourself off as soon as we finish making love." Paul stuffed his hands in his front pockets.

"I know better than to get too accustomed to the sex, guys. You'll get tired of me soon enough."

"We've had this conversation already. We're not going to get tired of you. We want you in our lives forever. We love you, Lana." Justin almost yelled the last out at her.

"No, you can't love me." She backed away from them only to find herself against the window.

"Why the hell not? You can't dictate whether we fall in love with you or not." Paul stalked toward her.

"You're out of my league, Paul. You and Justin are handsome and wealthy. You've got a successful business. I'm nobody. Why would you want to be associated with me?"

"That's enough, Lana! I don't want to hear you putting yourself down. There is nothing wrong with you. You're beautiful and caring. You're all we think about every minute of the day." Justin stared at her as his brother stopped directly in front of her.

"Is it because there are two of us? Are you embarrassed to be seen with two men around town?" Paul spat out the words as he grabbed her arms, jerking her against him.

"No! I mean, there are other ménage relationships here in Riverbend. I just can't see you being satisfied with me." She realized it really didn't matter that there were two of them. She could care less what anyone else thought.

Did they feel the same way? Could they actually not care that she was a nobody? She was nothing to look at and didn't have the slightest idea how to be someone they could be proud of. Could she risk taking a chance that they really did love her?

"Then why don't you want to believe that we really do care about you? Sweetheart, you're our everything. We don't want to even consider living the rest of our lives without you in it. Why do you think we didn't want you to move back into that damn apartment? We want you here with us." Justin smoothed a hand down her hair at the side of her face.

"I–I want to believe you."

"What's stopping you?"

"I don't know. It just seems too good to be true, too good to last."

"Give us a chance to prove it to you, baby. Let's go out for dinner tomorrow night after work. We'll take you to the steakhouse and just spend some time together." Paul released his grip on her arms.

"Um, let's wait and go Saturday night. That way none of us will have to get up early the next day to go to work." Lana couldn't believe she was actually considering their claim.

Then again, she might just be clinging to the chance of holding on to them for a little longer. It was too late for her heart. It was already fully engaged. She was headed for heartbreak and had no one to blame but herself. The only question was if her soul would survive intact or be torn apart at their eventual desertion.

* * * *

Justin followed Paul out to the truck. He couldn't believe that Lana still doubted their love for her and the fact that they were in it for keeps. Why would she doubt herself like that? Everything about her was so open and honest. She hadn't said the words yet, but both he and his brother knew she loved them. It was in her eyes whenever they made love to her. The way she smiled when they touched her left no doubt in his heart that she loved them as deeply as they loved her.

"Are you okay with waiting until Saturday night to take her out?" he asked his brother.

"Yeah. It's probably a good idea. I'm not going to want to let her free once I get my hands on her. We should take her dancing as well. The more we get her out with us in public, the sooner she'll accept that we're serious and not going to change our minds."

"I still think that part of her is worried about the ménage aspect." Justin pulled off his seat belt as they pulled up at the job site.

"Could be. Getting out in public with us should help alleviate some of that. There are enough ménage relationships here that she shouldn't feel self-conscious about it. We'll just have to make sure some of our friends are around as well."

They both climbed out of the truck and surveyed the work being completed. Justin made sure the sprinkler system was being installed according to his plans then pulled out his phone and made some return calls. It sure helped to have the phones rolling over to the office now. If it was an emergency, she would call them and relay the message. Now they weren't constantly being distracted by the phone while they were trying to concentrate at work.

Having her there at the office helping to keep things running smoothly was comforting in more ways than one. First, it meant she was safe at their house. Second, it meant she was close to them and easily accessible, and third, they had a better chance of seducing her into accepting them as her lovers and eventually, her husbands.

Not for the first time, Justin wondered if they should go ahead and ask her to marry them. Surely that would impress on her their sincerity where nothing else had so far. Paul seemed to think it was too soon. He'd argued that she would never accept such a quick proposal after only a few weeks. Maybe he was right. All Justin knew was that he wanted her in their home for good as well as in their bed. One without the other wasn't enough. He wouldn't settle for anything less than her entire commitment. He wanted it all.

It wasn't lost on him that part of her hesitation stemmed from the fact that she was used to being independent and taking care of herself. He and Paul, especially Paul, liked to take care of her and wanted to handle everything for her so she wouldn't have to worry about a thing. That wasn't going over very well with Lana. She valued being self-sufficient.

"What are you concentrating so hard on?" Paul's voice startled him.

He looked down at the pipe he'd been working with and realized he'd almost bent it too much. Shaking his head, Justin handed it off to one of the men setting the pipe and climbed out of the trench.

"You know, part of the problem with Lana is that she is stubbornly independent. She doesn't like having someone take the reins from her."

Paul nodded. "Yeah, I caught on to that, little brother. She's just going to have to get used to it. I like taking care of her."

"Me, too, but we're going to have to back off some, or she's just going to get her stubborn on and make things even more difficult."

"Just thinking about her being stubborn has my hand itching to redden her bottom." Paul's grin was infectious.

Justin shook his head. There was no compromise with his brother when it came to being in charge. He tended to take over everything he had a hand in and run it. Somehow Justin didn't think it was going to work that well with Lana. Her stubborn streak was just as strong as Paul's. He could foresee a lot of fireworks in their future. He chuckled. As long as they had a future, he would take the fireworks and be the one to cool them off when needed. Somehow the idea of Lana all fired up got his blood pumping and his dick jumping. He couldn't wait for Saturday night.

Chapter Eighteen

Saturday morning arrived sooner than Lana expected. The previous workweek had been busy. Between learning new things and trying to keep her distance from the brothers, she wasn't sure how she managed to make it. Justin and Paul both teased her every chance they got, keeping her on her toes and in a constant state of arousal that made it nearly impossible to concentrate.

She had managed to finish up and leave on Friday afternoon before they made it home so there had been no chance that they would try and talk her into spending the night. She knew they had to work today. She half expected them to call her the night before, but they hadn't, and a part of her had been disappointed. In a little over two weeks she had gotten accustomed to having them around her and missed them when they weren't.

Lana rushed through her house chores then made out a grocery list and drove to the store. She spent nearly an hour just wandering around town, looking in windows at some of the interesting things. She wanted to explore a few of the shops, but decided to wait until she actually had the money to spend.

Just as she turned back to head to the grocery store, Lana ran into Beth. The other woman hugged her before she even realized what she was going to do.

"How are you doing? I'm so glad to see you. It's a miracle that you weren't seriously hurt the other night."

"Hey, Beth. I'm fine. How are you doing?" Lana wasn't sure what to say to the other woman.

"How are Paul and Justin treating you? Mac said they were fit to be tied when they got to the hospital that night."

"Um, they've been very nice to me." Lana felt the heat crawl up her neck into her face.

"Mac said you're working for them now. How do you like it?" Beth's curiosity seemed friendly enough, but Lana was uncomfortable.

As if picking up on this, Beth took her elbow and urged her toward the coffee shop on the corner.

"Let's have a cup of coffee and visit. I love having someone to talk to when I get out of the house. I spend so much time inside working that when I do talk myself into getting out I want someone to talk to."

Lana took a seat at one of the outdoor tables. Almost immediately a young woman greeted them and took their order. Beth sighed and leaned back in the chair.

"Did you ever get to download the books I loaned you through Kindle?"

"Yes, I did. I've read several of them and really enjoyed them. Thanks. I can't believe people actually write that stuff." Once again her face began to heat up.

Lana quickly looked around to see if anyone was paying any attention to them. She wasn't surprised to see a threesome walking out of the leather shop down the street hand in hand. Ménage relationships seemed to be fairly popular in Riverbend. Though she had been aware of it before, having been with both Justin and Paul, she seemed to notice it much more.

"I love to read a good love story when there is some action involved. Of course, it doesn't hurt when the sex is nice and raunchy, either." Beth winked at her.

"How long have you and your husbands been together?"

The waitress returned with their coffee and Danish orders. After taking a sip of her coffee, Beth answered her question.

"Over a year now. They are the best things that ever happened to me. I had known them for most of my life, but I had moved off for several years. When I moved back, it seemed like they were always close by. Then I got into some trouble last year and they went all protective over me. Sort of like how Justin and Paul are doing with you."

"Yeah, they don't like where I live and are all over me to move in with them. I don't think it's a good idea for me to get too involved with them, though."

"Why not?" Beth looked confused. "They obviously care a lot about you. You can see it in their eyes when they look at you."

"They're out of my league. I can't compete with the type of women they are probably used to."

"Now listen here, Lana. Don't think for one minute that you're not important to them. They wouldn't be pursuing you if they weren't serious. Why would you think they are better than you are?"

Lana sighed and studied her coffee. "I barely manage to pay my bills, and sometimes I have to really scrimp to do it. I'm nothing special to look at and don't know the first thing about how to dress up to look like a lady. They're worldly and have money. They could have the pick of any woman out there. I can't believe they won't get tired of me."

Beth just shook her head. "Nonsense. They picked you. You didn't throw yourself at them. Cut yourself some slack. Those men wouldn't be spending time with you if they didn't truly want to. No one forces men like them or my men into doing something they don't want to do."

"I hope you're right. I love my job. I really don't want to lose it because I made the mistake of screwing the bosses."

"So what are you doing tonight? Have plans?"

"Actually, they asked me out to eat. I think we're going to the steakhouse."

"Wonderful! Maybe you will end up going out to dance afterward. I think Mac and Mason are going to take me out tonight. Maybe we will see each other then."

They finished up their coffee and Danish then parted ways. Lana's brief talk with Beth gave her hope that maybe things would work out with her men. Maybe she was being too hard on herself after all. She quickly finished up shopping and hurried home to unpack the groceries. She wanted to spend the afternoon pampering herself. She would take a nice long bath and shave her legs. Then she would wash her hair and paint her nails.

Just as she got out of the tub, her phone rang. Lana answered after noting that it was Justin's number.

"Hello?"

"Hey, sweetheart. How are you doing today?"

"I'm fine. Did you have a busy day today?"

"We got a lot accomplished. We got an early start, so we're heading home now to shower and dress for our night out. How about if we pick you up about six thirty?"

Lana felt her belly flutter. She couldn't stop the surge of excitement that it was nearly time for them to be together once again. She tamped down the rush of happiness and tempered her response.

"That would be fine. I should be ready by then."

"Have you been busy today?"

"Just housework and shopping. Nothing major."

"Did you think about us?" Justin's voice dipped lower.

Something about the deeper timbre pulled at her womb as if there was a direct line to her clit. She fought to keep from sighing into the phone.

"I suppose I did some."

He growled into the phone. "Don't tease me, Lana. I'll take it out on you later."

"Promises." She popped her hand over her mouth. Where had that come from?

He chuckled. "Okay. Get ready for us. We'll see you soon. Paul said for you to expect a spanking for teasing us."

Before she could answer him, Justin had hung up. She frowned at the phone. She couldn't believe she had acted like a seductress to them. And why did the threat of a spanking have her panties wet all of a sudden? She wouldn't let Paul spank her. Would she?

Lana washed her hair and dried it before slipping into a pantsuit that was a deep emerald green. She found a pair of strappy sandals and left them by the couch to put on later. She had just started applying makeup when someone knocked on her door. She checked the time and frowned. It was still too early for it to be Paul and Justin. She peeked through the peephole and recognized Rick. What was he doing there?

She unlocked the door and opened it just wide enough to be friendly but not wide enough to invite him inside. His eyes widened when he saw her.

"Hey, Lana. How are you doing? I've been worried about you since your attack." He looked at where her hand held the door. "Um, can I come in?"

"I don't think that's a good idea, Rick. I'm getting ready to go out. Can I help you with something?"

"Can't I just come by to check on you? I was upset that you had gotten hurt and then you just disappeared for a while."

"I was staying with Justin and Paul. You know that."

"Yeah, people have been talking about it, too. I was hoping you would have dinner with me tonight. I thought maybe we could talk."

"About what, Rick? You made it clear that you think I'm a slut because I stayed with them. You as much as told me that my reputation was ruined. Why would you want to be seen with me now?"

"I didn't say that exactly. Besides, I can forgive you because you were hurt and needed somewhere safe to stay. I think people will cut you some slack after what happened." Rick tried to crowd the door.

"I don't care what they think. All that matters is what I think. Justin and Paul have been very good to me when I needed help. I owe them for all of their help."

"So that's why you're sleeping with them." Rick sneered.

"It's none of your business. Go on, Rick, and leave me alone." She tried to shut the door, but Rick stuck his foot in the door.

"Not yet. I'm not finished with you." He shoved at the door and managed to get it to move another few inches. "If you owe anyone, it's me, Lana. I gave you a job when I didn't have to. I think you've got your priorities a little out of order."

Lana fought to get the door to close, but Rick was a big man just like Justin and Paul were. He wasn't going to be moved if he didn't want to go.

"Get out, Rick. I don't know what you think you're doing, but you need to leave. I don't owe you anything but my thanks. I worked hard while I worked at The Burger Hop."

"Yeah, but you wouldn't go out with me. Why are you seeing them? It's disgusting to let them share you between them like that."

"Rick! What in the hell are you doing here?" Paul's deep voice sent a shiver of relief through her.

* * * *

Rick was pulled out of the doorway, and Justin's body blocked the door. Lana struggled to see around him to find out what was going on.

"I have just as much right to be here as you do. I wanted to see how she was doing after the attack."

"She's fine. We're taking care of her. You need to leave. Now."

"That's not up to you. I'm not going anywhere until she says so."

"Lana? Tell Rick you don't want to see him." Paul's voice held a thread of agitation that tightened her stomach.

"Paul, it's okay. Rick was just leaving. Don't do anything crazy, Paul. Justin, move so I can see."

"Just stay where you are, Lana." Justin didn't move an inch from his spot in front of the door.

"Lana, don't listen to them. They're only going to hurt you in the long run. They never stay with anyone more than a few months." Rick sounded almost desperate now.

"Shut the fuck up, Rick. Get out of here. You don't know what you're talking about." Justin spoke up this time.

"I'm leaving, Lana. Don't expect me to pick up the pieces when they get finished with you." She heard him curse then stomp off down the sidewalk.

Justin moved out of the doorway. Both he and Paul stared down at her with concern in their eyes.

"Did he hurt you, baby?" Paul reached out and touched the side of her face.

"No, he was just talking to me. Nothing happened." Lana backed up and let them in. "I'm almost ready. Give me a minute."

"Take all the time you need, sweetheart." Justin walked over to the loveseat and sat down.

She quickly finished her light makeup then returned to the living area to slip into her sandals. Grabbing her purse, she smiled shyly at Paul and held out her arms.

"Will I do?"

"You'll do wonderfully. Are you ready?"

"Whenever you are."

Justin took her hand in his and led her to the door. Paul closed and locked the door behind them. She was surprised to find that Justin was driving for a change. This left Paul free to tease and torment her. He kissed her lightly on the lips then squeezed her thigh after buckling them both in.

"You smell good enough to eat, like vanilla and cinnamon." Paul leaned over and buried his face in her hair before kissing her once more.

Justin kept both hands on the wheel, but he stole quick glances at them from time to time. Paul's fingers curled a strand of hair around them and he tugged on it. The hand on her leg moved up and down in a sensual slide that had her pussy on high alert. When he brushed a single finger against the apex of her legs, Lana though for sure she would cry out in a quick release. Somehow she managed to tighten down on her libido. If he kept teasing her though, she had little doubt she would be coming in the truck on the way to dinner.

"Paul. Stop it."

"Stop what, babe? Stop loving on you? Not going to happen. I like touching you."

"You're making me uncomfortable."

Justin chuckled, and she shot him a scowl. He didn't seem the least worried about it.

"I like it when you're antsy. It tells me that you want me. Do you want my cock in your pussy, Lana?"

"Paul!" She leaned her head back against the seat and closed her eyes as his fingers grazed lightly over her crotch.

Two could play at that game. She reached over and raked her nails over Paul's bulge, enjoying the rasp of her nails against the jeans material.

"Fuck! Do that again, baby, and I'll take you right here in this truck."

"We're almost there, Paul." Justin's smiling voice interrupted her self-imposed fantasy of Paul fucking her in the back seat.

"You hold that thought, Lana. Whatever it was, it looked like something I want to be a part of." Justin grinned over at her as he pulled into the parking lot of the steakhouse.

Paul had her seat belt off and the door open in no time. He helped her out of the truck, and the three of them walked together up to the door. Before they could open the door, someone beat them to it and held the door for them.

"Well, hey there, Paul, Justin. Who do you have with you?"

"Randy, this is Lana. Lana, this is Randy Woods and his brother, Travis. Coming through the door there is Marx."

Lana stepped back into Paul's body. The two men were huge, and there was an air of authority about them that she couldn't place.

"It's a pleasure to meet you, Lana. Don't let those two corrupt you." Randy smiled at her.

"Shut up, Randy." Paul all but growled.

Travis nodded at them. "Heard you finally managed to talk someone into having pity on you two and taking on that office position."

"Lana's doing an excellent job." Justin sounded proud of her.

"Randy and Travis own a ranch outside of town. We've done a little work for them in the past." Justin grinned down at her where she was standing almost on top of Paul.

"Pleased to meet you." She looked up at both men for a brief second then dropped her eyes back to her feet.

Something about them intimidated her to the point that she didn't want to get too close to them. Paul seemed to enjoy the fact that she was all but climbing up his body. The four men exchanged a few more words then Travis and Randy moved on.

"Did they make you nervous, Lana?" Paul asked with just a hint of a smile.

Lana scowled at him. Justin chuckled as they followed a waitress to their table. They each ordered something to drink then looked over the menu. She realized she was starved as she glanced over the selections. It didn't take her long to settle on smoked chicken and a salad with honey mustard dressing.

Both men chose steaks with baked potatoes. They settled into an easy conversation about work and what they would be working on next now that the sprinkler system was nearly finished. By the time they had finished their meal, Lana felt much better about going out with them. They had eased her into feeling comfortable around them.

"Would you let us take you dancing at the bar now?" Justin asked.

"Dancing sounds like fun. I ran into Beth this morning and she said they might be going out tonight."

"Sounds like we might have a crowd, then. We better get going or we won't be able to get a table."

"I'd just as soon we didn't have a crowd. I don't want to have to fight anyone to keep them away from Lana." Paul's dark eyes held the promise of heat within them.

"Somehow I don't think anyone is going to want to fight you for me."

She knew it was the wrong thing to say even as the words left her mouth. Both men rounded on her in the parking lot and backed her up against the truck.

Chapter Nineteen

"What are you talking about?" Justin leaned in on one side of her with a hand on the side of the truck.

Paul moved in on the other side of her, caging her in with his body. She had nowhere to go now. Both men looked angry. She wasn't really scared of them, but she couldn't help the little hiccup of worry.

"I–I just mean that I doubt anyone will bother me." She wrung her hands as they continued to stare at her.

"I think you're quickly adding up your punishment, Lana. We won't let you talk bad about yourself. Do you understand?" Paul ran a finger along her lower lip.

"P–Punishment?"

"You've earned a nice little spanking, babe. I can't wait to feel your sweet ass heat up under my hand."

Lana shivered despite the warm temperature. The idea of getting a spanking had her clenching her thighs together. She was sure her panties were soaked by now. Why would getting whipped turn her on? Maybe because it was Paul who was going to spank her and she knew how that would end.

"I think she's looking forward to it, Paul. Her eyes are all shiny." Justin leaned in and gave her a quick, hard kiss. "We better hurry up."

Paul pulled her into his arms and lifted her up onto the seat of the truck. Then he scooted in next to her. It didn't take long to drive the short distance to the bar. The street in front of the building was already lined with cars. She wondered how there would be enough room inside the building for all the people it suggested would be in there.

Almost as soon as they walked through the doors, people were greeting them on all sides. Lana recognized some from the party at Beth's house and some from The Burger Hop. Everyone seemed friendly enough. She slowly relaxed.

"Hey, Lana! Over here!"

She recognized Beth's voice, though she couldn't see her very well around the group of men blocking her view. She started to pull away from Paul, but he held tightly to her.

"Where are you going?" he asked.

"Beth is calling me. I'll be right over there." She pointed in the general direction she'd heard the other woman's voice come from.

He looked over and nodded. "Don't go anywhere else. We'll be right there."

She smiled and hurried around the men to locate her friend. She hoped that there would be more women that she knew there tonight. The prospect of being surrounded by so many men was overwhelming. Sure enough, sitting next to Beth was Lexie. Both women stood up and hugged her.

"I'm so glad you're here. Caitlyn and her sister-in-law, Tish, will be here soon." Beth pulled a chair closer to them at the table.

"Hi, Lana. How are you doing?" Mason, one of Beth's husbands, walked up and kissed the top of Beth's head.

"I'm fine, thanks." She smiled at how he watched Beth fondly.

"I think I see Tish and Caitlyn's crew coming through the door now, ladies." Mason nodded toward the front of the bar.

"Oh, good! Make sure they make it back here, Mason."

He smiled at them and walked toward the front of the building. Beth took a drink of her beer.

"Lexie is reading the latest Tymber Dalton book. She says it's beyond hot! I can't wait. I've been too busy to read lately. I'm going to try to get to it tomorrow though." She winked at them.

"How are things going with Justin and Paul?" Lexie asked.

"I love working for them. The job is fun but challenging."

"That's not quite what I meant, honey." Lexie winked at her.

"Oh! Well, um, everything is fine, I guess." She felt her face growing warm.

"Don't feel embarrassed with us, sweetie. We're all in the same boat." Beth giggled.

"Hey, everyone!" Tish walked up pulling Caitlyn along with her.

"Hey, Tish, Caitlyn. Grab a chair and have a seat. I have a feeling the guys are going to be busy for a while." Beth waved the two women over to join them.

They spent the next thirty minutes talking about everything from what they were reading to their sex life, much to Lana's amazement. They didn't seem the least bit embarrassed to talk about anything around each other.

"You'll get used to it, Lana. Everyone is open and honest around here. We don't gossip, just share our lives." Tish smiled at her.

"Everyone here looks out for each other. If you ever need anything, you can count on one of us to help you." Lexie winked at Beth.

"What are you ladies up to over here?" Brian Southworth asked as he, Andy Kent, and Mason Tidwell walked up and pulled chairs up to the table around their wives.

"Just catching up, Brian. Where are the other Neanderthals?" Beth asked with a grin.

"Getting beer. There's a line at the bar a mile long." Andy twirled a strand of his wife's hair around his finger.

Slowly the group enlarged until one side of the bar contained the ménage society of Riverbend, Texas. Lana couldn't get over how nice everyone was. There were nearly twelve of them there that she knew and several others she didn't.

Justin handed her a drink and picked her up to sit in his lap as Paul took a chair next to her. They all talked over each other until the band started playing. Then the dance floor filled up.

"We'll take the next song, sweetheart." Justin nipped at her earlobe.

She scrunched up her neck and popped his arm. "Stop that."

"Nope. I like gnawing on you."

"But we're in public, Justin. Someone will see you."

"So look over at what Mac's doing to Beth."

Lana glanced across the table to see Mac's hand rubbing between the other woman's legs. She jerked her eyes back and shivered. Justin chuckled in her ear.

"See."

"It doesn't mean you have to do it." She hoped he didn't stop.

Several minutes later, Paul grabbed her from Justin's lap and led her to the dance floor. It was crowded to the point that about all they could do was hold on and sway to the music. Paul's knee pressed between her legs and rubbed at her crotch.

"Oh, God."

"You like that, don't you?"

She could only moan as he licked her neck then nibbled along her jaw. The next thing she knew, Justin had eased in behind her and was pressing his hardened cock against her ass. Stuck between them, it was all she could do to keep from going up in smoke there on the dance floor. They were teasing her beyond her control.

"I can't wait to get you home. We're going to fuck that sweet ass and that wet pussy until you scream our names. Then we're going to do it all again." Paul's deep, rich voice tightened things deep inside her.

"I can't wait to suck your nipples and watch them get hard for me. I could play with those little berries for hours." Justin's hot breath played along the back of her neck.

Finally the song ended, and they escorted her back to the tables where the group had congregated. She wanted to fan herself, but didn't dare draw attention to her condition. It wouldn't take much, and Lana was sure she would climax in front of God and everybody.

"Lana. Want to make a bathroom trip with us?" Beth grabbed her hand.

"Yes!" Relief poured over her like a cool glass of water.

They excused themselves and she followed Beth, Lexie, and Tish toward the other side of the bar where the bathrooms where located. Justin had squeezed her hand as she left, reminding her to hurry back. She was secretly thankful for the brief reprieve. They were getting to her.

"Man, Paul and Justin are really pouring it on, aren't they?" Tish grinned at her as she touched up her lipstick.

"I don't know what's gotten into them." Lana washed her hands.

"They're seducing you, honey. You've been holding back on them and they want to make sure you know where they stand." Beth's eyes met hers in the mirror. "They love you, Lana. Do you love them?"

Panic had her heart stuttering. How should she answer that?

"Never mind. I can see it in your eyes. You love them just as much as they love you."

"I–I don't think you're right about them loving me, though. I think they really care about me, but maybe 'love' is too strong a word for it."

Lexie chuckled. "Lana, there's no way to mistake what they feel for you as anything but love. They can't keep their eyes off of you. Don't screw it up, honey. Tell them how you feel."

"But what if it doesn't last?" she whispered, wringing her hands.

Fear of finding out that they were wrong almost paralyzed her. What would she do if she bared her soul to them and they really didn't feel the same way? How would she ever be able to continue working for them? How would she be able to be near them and know that it hadn't been real?

"You have to take that chance, Lana. I can't imagine them ever falling out of love with you considering how they follow you with their eyes. We all had to take that chance when we confessed that we loved our men. Don't let fear spoil the best thing you will ever have in your life. There's nothing like the love of two men to get you through life's ups and downs."

"We better get back out there before they come looking for us." Beth took Lana's hand and squeezed it. "Don't get hung up on the little things, girl. You'll pick everything to death. Now let's go have some fun."

The second they stepped out of the bathroom, Lana knew the men were watching her. She could feel their eyes on her and let Beth's and Tish's words sink in. She'd never had even one man pay as much attention to her as both Justin and Paul did. It was a little overwhelming and exciting at the same time.

"Feeling okay, babe?" Paul took her hand and pulled her into his arms.

"Yeah, I'm fine." She smiled and allowed herself to relax a little more into his arms.

"How about another dance?" He led her out on the floor and wrapped himself around her.

His scent washed over her as she buried her face in his chest. She let the soft melody of the music flow through her as she allowed herself to finally enjoy just being with Paul for those few minutes. How could she possibly ignore the way they made her feel? Yes, Paul could be controlling and exasperating at times, but he truly cared about her and wanted what was best for her.

When the song ended, Justin was there to take over the next dance. Paul kissed her lightly on the lips and left her in his brother's arms. She snuggled into him and reveled in the warmth of his skin and the way he hummed the words against her ear. Justin would always have a smile for her and would buffer Paul's overprotective tendencies.

Deep down, Lana knew she couldn't stop loving them and if one day they changed their minds, she wouldn't regret one moment with them. They were hers forever, and she was going to grab hold of what they were offering with both hands. Now that she'd made up her mind, she couldn't wait to tell them, but she didn't want to do it in a bar or in the truck. She wanted to tell them in private when they could all hold each other. She couldn't wait to be alone with them, but she wasn't going to cut the night short, either. She was having too much fun being among friends and learning what it was like to have them.

"What's that I see in your eye, Lana?" Justin stared down at her as the music stopped.

"Hmm, I don't know. Maybe happiness?"

"It looks good on you. Having fun, sweetheart?"

"All because of you and Paul." She stood up on her toes and kissed him on the chin.

"What was that for?"

"For caring about me. For being you."

He chuckled and wrapped an arm around her as he moved them through the crowd back to their tables. When they approached, Paul stood up and gave her his seat. Then he rested his hands on her shoulders as he continued his conversation with Mac and Brian.

She listened in to the conversations going on around her between the various subgroups around the tables. When Caitlyn brought up the subject of children, everyone at both tables went silent. Lamar's and Brody's eyes got wide.

"Are you trying to tell us something, baby?" Brody asked.

"No! I was just asking Beth when they were going to think about kids. I wasn't talking to you two at all."

Lana smothered a smile. Poor Caitlyn's face had pinked up into a nice bright color. Everyone stared at Beth, Mac, and Mason now.

"Don't look at me. I'm not pregnant." Beth frowned at poor Caitlyn.

Then everyone dissolved into laughter and the mood was broken. Lana had never enjoyed herself more. She knew that she could depend on any of those women if she ever needed someone to talk to.

"Ready to go, babe?" Paul leaned over her shoulder and whispered into her ear.

"Yeah, whenever you two are ready. This has been fun, but I'm tired."

"Come on, Justin. Lana is tired."

Justin walked over and took her hand. "We're heading out, everyone. This has been fun. We need to have another party before winter gets here and it's too cold to be outside."

"We'll have it at our place next time," Paul told them.

Justin's quick look let Lana know that this was something exceptional for Paul to have volunteered their home.

"See you all later." They all said good-bye and waved as the men escorted her toward the door.

Once outside in the still-warm night, Lana drew in a deep breath. It had been stuffy in the bar with so many people crowded in one spot.

"Did you have a good time?" Justin opened the door to the truck and helped her up into the cab.

"I had a great time. Everyone is so nice."

"Nothing like good friends you can depend on." Paul climbed up on the other side of the truck and started the engine.

"Lana, we want you to come home with us tonight. Will you do that?" Paul drew her hand to his lips.

"I'd like that. I'd like that a lot."

Chapter Twenty

The second they were in the house, Paul had Lana in his arms and was striding for the bedroom. He couldn't wait one more second to have her naked in their bed. He could feel Justin close behind him. Lana was a comfortable weight in his arms as he hurried up the stairs. He only hoped he didn't embarrass himself before he got inside of her. His cock was throbbing with need, pressed so tight against his zipper that he figured he would have a bruise.

He pushed open the door to the bedroom with his foot and left its closure to his brother. He was too intent on getting Lana naked and beneath him. Her musky scent called to him. He knew she was soaking wet between her legs and couldn't wait to taste her sweet ambrosia. There was no patience left in him. Paul jerked her blouse open, sending buttons flying as he pulled it off her arms. Then Justin was there, fiddling with the clasp to her bra.

Paul went to work on unfastening her jeans and pulling off her shoes so he could get the stiff material out of his way. At last, all that was left was the flimsy material of her panties, damp from her juices.

"God, I can smell your cunt, ripe and ready for us. Please tell me you want us, Lana."

"I want you, Paul. I want you both."

He watched her eyes darken as he jerked his shirt over his head with one hand and dropped it. Then he unfastened his jeans and toed off his boots. He heard the unmistakable sound of a zipper and knew that Justin was way ahead of him. He shucked his jeans and boxers all at one time before kneeling on the bed next to his sweet Lana.

"Look at her, Justin. Look at how much she wants us. Her pussy is weeping."

Paul moved up her body to stare into her heavy-lidded eyes. They watched him with enough emotion in them to assure him that she loved them. She might not have said it yet, but it was there in her eyes. He sipped at her lips as his brother lay down on the other side of her. They were plump and soft against his. When he licked along the seam, she moaned and opened to him.

Everything poured out of him and into her as he tried to tell her in that kiss just how much she meant to him. He stroked his tongue along hers then explored her mouth before drawing back and nibbling at her lower lip.

Lana moaned against his mouth and arched her back. He was sure Justin was making love to her breasts by the way she was moving. The thought of those luscious berries had him kissing and nipping his way down her jaw and across her neck. He stopped to suck at the juncture of her neck and shoulder. He loved the way she reacted when he touched her there. The idea of leaving his mark there had him sucking a bit harder. Then he moved farther down and joined his brother at her breasts.

Justin moved his hand out of the way so that Paul could latch on to the nipple on his side. He sucked and pulled on the tight bud even as his brother tended to the other one. Lana's fingers dug into his scalp. The sharp pricks drew a growl from his throat as he tried to stuff as much of her breast as he could into his mouth. Pulling away, he lapped at the underside of the voluptuous mound before kissing his way down her abdomen to her pelvis.

"Oh, God! Please."

Paul stopped licking and kissing long enough to ask her what she needed.

"More. I need more."

Paul chuckled and licked over the sensitive spot at her groin before returning to her belly button and rimming it with his tongue.

She tried moving her body to align his mouth up with her clit. He easily avoided her manipulations as he made his way there in his own time.

The instant his tongue traced over her pussy lips, Paul felt pre-cum seep from his dick. He ground his cock into the bed in an attempt to regain control. It didn't help. He sucked on her before pulling back and blowing against the wet tissue. He heard her gasp and smiled before returning to the delicacy of her juicy cunt.

The more he sucked and licked, the harder she bucked against him. He pressed one hand down on her pelvis to try and control her movements. When he stabbed her pussy with his tongue, she screamed out and jerked again.

"Help me keep her still, Justin."

His brother added a hand to hold her down while continuing to play and suck on her breasts. The swollen berries were elongated and dark with the heat of her arousal.

Paul returned to torturing her with his tongue, teeth, and fingers. Spreading her pussy lips wide, he licked all along the slit from top to bottom and then back up again. He drew a circle around her clit without touching it and grinned at the creative curses flowing from her mouth. He chuckled against her wet heat. He still owed her a spanking. They might not get to it tonight, but they would get to it eventually. All he could do right now was worship her body with his.

When he slipped a finger inside her cunt, she moaned and tried to trap it there using her tight muscles. He stroked it in and out of her several times before adding a second finger and curling around to locate her hot spot. She called out his name when he rasped over the sensitive tissues. Taking advantage of it, Paul pressed on it over and over until she was begging for him to fuck her. Her breathy demands had his cock aching even more than it had been. He had to have her.

"Justin. Move."

His brother let go of the nipple he had been sucking on with a loud pop and moved out of the way. Paul rolled off of the bed and grabbed a condom from the bedside table. He tore it open and rolled it over his straining cock in one quick move. Then he lay back on the bed.

"Ride me, Lana. My dick is so fucking hard I can't take a full breath." He held out his arms for her.

Lana climbed up on him and slowly sank down over his cock as he held it steady for her. As her pussy sucked him inside, Paul knew it was where he wanted to be. She groaned as she fought to accommodate his thick width. Even as wet as she was, it was a tight fit. He had to grit his teeth to keep from coming the second he was fully seated. He held her still when she tried to move.

"No. Not yet, babe. I need a minute."

"Please, Paul. I need you."

"Justin. She's so fucking tight. I can't hold on for long." It felt so good it was almost painful as she squeezed around him. He was sure there were stars exploding behind his eyelids.

* * * *

Justin could hear the strain in his brother's voice as he tried to hold on to his sanity. He pressed gently against Lana's back to position her over his brother's chest so he could reach her ass. In this position the little star winked at him as her pussy was stretched around Paul's cock. He donned a condom then spread a generous amount of lube down her ass. Gently massaging the slippery stuff against her back hole, it flexed around him. Just the sight of it flexing had his dick jerking against his belly.

He slowly pushed his finger at the opening and held his breath as the tiny hole opened for him. He managed to get it to the first knuckle. Slowly, he pushed it in and out until he had his entire finger deep inside her back entrance. Adding more lube, he added a second finger and felt her squeeze against him this time.

"Easy, Lana. Just relax and push out." Even he could hear the strain in his voice. She might be stretching to accommodate him, but he was pushed to go slow.

Once he managed to get both fingers all the way inside of her, Justin slowly fucked her with the two appendages until she was pushing back against him. He could feel his brother's cock through the thin membrane separating both passages. He couldn't wait to feel that tight hole closing around his cock.

"Hurry up, Justin." Sweat beaded on his forehead as he withdrew his fingers and added more lube before greasing it over his sheathed cock.

Justin pressed the head of his cock against her dark rosette and pushed. For just an instant, she clamped down, refusing him entrance. Then she relaxed and his dick slowly began to make some headway until finally, it popped through the tightly resistant ring.

"Oh, God! It's too much."

"Do I need to stop, Lana?" Justin prayed she wouldn't ask him to, but he would if he was hurting her. The last thing he ever wanted to do was cause her harm.

"No. Hurry. I can't handle it. I'm so full!"

Justin pressed forward and felt the tight tissues give way until he was balls-deep inside her ass. A burning heat seared his dick as he slowly pulled out and then tunneled back in. He felt Paul pull out and then push in as he retreated. They set up a slow, steady rhythm that threatened to unman him. His balls were already drawn tight against his body as he slowly increased the rate of his lunging in and out of her. Between his and Paul's plunges, Lana began to tremble all over. He wasn't sure if it was with pain or ecstasy. He gritted his teeth against the need to come. He could tell his brother was having the same issues.

"Are you okay, sweetheart?"

"Yes! Fuck me! Harder. I need to come." She thrashed between them now as she fought her release.

"Let it go, baby." Paul's voice sounded tight and far away.

"It's too much. I won't be able to live through it."

"We've got you, Lana. Let go."

Finally, he felt her explode around him. Her ass milked his cock until his strangled cry joined her scream and his brother's muffled shout. They all three came together. His cock jerked deep inside of her and then he collapsed over her, managing to hold himself up with one arm.

"Fuck!" Justin's strangled cry had him slowly pulling out of Lana's sweet ass.

He disposed of the condom and wet a cloth with warm water to clean their woman's sweaty body. He liked taking care of her. He would run a bath for her soon. Right now, he just wanted to curl around her. As soon as he had her cleaned off, Justin pulled her over to curl into his arms while Paul drew out of her and tended to his condom as well. Then they both spooned with her as the slick sweat cooled on their bodies. Never had he felt so close to another human being as he did when they had all three been joined by her body. He'd felt a little bit of heaven in those brief moments while they were wide open and vulnerable. He felt love pour between them and knew without a doubt that she was theirs.

* * * *

Lana fought to regain her composure as she slowly caught her breath. She had no doubt in her mind that Paul and Justin loved her or that they were right for her. She felt as if a small piece of their souls now resided inside of her. An overwhelming peace settled over her.

She snuggled into Paul's back even as she pulled Justin's arm tighter around her. This was what she had been craving—a home where she felt loved and needed. She wanted to be a part of them even as she helped make them into a family. She could do that without losing her independence with their help. Paul would constantly challenge her but not because he wanted to control her. She now knew he wanted only to take care of her and keep her safe. With Justin's help, they would forge a compromise that would work for all three of them.

The feel of their skin against hers grounded her in the here and now. She felt as if without their touch she would float away with happiness. Lana kissed Paul's shoulder and hugged him tighter.

"I love you, Paul. I need you so much."

"Baby, you're my life. I'll always love you."

"Justin, I love you, too. You make me so happy."

"Lana, I don't want to ever think about being without you. I love you."

Paul turned back toward her and cupped her cheek in his hand. The love she saw in his eyes brought tears to hers.

"Marry us, Lana. Be our wife and let us love you for the rest of our lives."

Justin squeezed her tighter. "You'll marry Paul on paper and then we'll have a ceremony with our friends where you marry us both. Say yes, baby."

Lana turned to her back and gazed into Justin's eyes then back to Paul. Her heart swelled with love. No doubts marred her mind as she smiled.

"Yes. I'll marry you both. I love you both so much."

They kissed her until she thought she would die for lack of oxygen, passing her back and forth between them until they finally fell asleep holding her.

She closed her eyes and promised herself that she would never doubt their love. If ever she had fears, she would go to them and talk to them about it. She trusted that their bond was forever. It had taken time for her to relax and accept that she had something to offer them other than her skills in the office. She had all of her love to give them, and in return, she took all of their love into her. Nothing could have ever prepared her for what to expect when two men set their sights on her, but right now, all she cared about was that they were all hers, forever and always.

THE END

WWW.MARLAMONROE.COM

ABOUT THE AUTHOR

Marla Monroe has been writing professionally for about ten years now. Her first book with Siren was published in January of 2011. She loves to write and spends every spare minute either at the keyboard or reading another Siren author. She writes everything from sizzling-hot contemporary cowboys to science-fiction ménages with the occasional badass biker thrown in for good measure.

Marla lives in the southern US and works full time at a busy hospital. When not writing, she loves to travel, spend time with her cats, and read. She's always eager to try something new and especially enjoys the research for her books. She loves to hear from readers about what they are looking for next.

You can reach Marla at themarlamonroe@yahoo.com or visit her website at www.marlamonroe.com.

For all titles by Marla Monroe, please visit
www.bookstrand.com/marla-monroe

Siren Publishing, Inc.
www.SirenPublishing.com